Nell Didn't Do It

Was it the poacher who operated near the dude ranch?

"We appreciate all tips on suspicious behavior," Officer Lester said, "since any one of them could lead to the apprehension of poachers."

I sucked in my breath. *Poachers!*

Or was it the moose?

"Wait a minute," said Andrea with a gulp, as if she'd swallowed her gum, "are you saying that moose we saw up there *killed* him?"

"Well, ma'am," Gustafson said, "we can't rightly say, but it looks like something trampled him. And we know that moose are in the area. Are you the one who reported the moose sighting?"

Andrea shook her head and looked at me. "Not me. It was *her*." She pointed her finger at me.

Also by Sue Star

Murder for a Cash Crop
Murder with Altitude
Murder in the Dojo
Dancing for the General (with Bill Beatty)

What the Critics Say About *Murder for a Cash Crop*:

There's a cinematic quality to this fast-paced, straightforward, easily digestible thriller, and it's worth a read just to get close to the clever, "positively old-fashioned" Nell, who though out of touch as she might be, is an admirable, and relatable protagonist...

A lighthearted, formulaic, but ultimately satisfying mystery novel with a charming heroine.

Kirkus Review

Murder by Moose

Sue Star

D. M. Kreg Publishing

DMKregPublishing.com

Cover Design: Renee Barratt, The Cover Counts

For Al, as always.

Acknowledgments

Thanks to the many fine martial artists with whom I've trained, and especially, thanks to Mr. Reid. Thanks also to the writers who helped this project along the way. The Boulder Lunch Bunch first encouraged me to write about Nell. Special thanks to the Inklings, my awesome critique group who help with countless details, and to the Oregon Writers Network, whose support keeps my career on track. Thanks to my first readers who rearranged their schedules to accommodate mine, and to my family for always humoring me and believing in me. Thanks to my editor, Lyn Worthen, and to my publisher, Donald Kreg. This book wouldn't have happened without any of you.

Murder by Moose

Sue Star

Chapter One

Pop— Pop—

It had started as an idyllic picnic. Sun warmed my face. Lake water lapped at my feet. Aspen leaves rustled in the breeze. My potential students and I had been chattering innocently, getting to know each other. I'd been talking up the benefits of martial arts, since I really needed to recruit these people. I was facing the looming threat of possible unemployment.

The four of us perched atop a cluster of boulders overlooking the postcard backdrop of mountain gold. I was savoring a homemade bun that the ranch's cook—and most importantly, *not* me—had packed for our lunch and wondering how much better could it get for a wronged suburban housewife turned ninja super mom like me, Nell Letterly? That's when two sharp pops split the air.

And they hadn't come from champagne corks.

They were gunshots.

"Take cover!" Harlan shouted, as he slid off his rock into a crouch beside its granite bulk.

Andrea, the bubbling, petite pixie, and her shy opposite, Libby, both squealed and dove next to him. They cowered there like children in a thunderstorm rather than the twenty-somethings I knew them to be from their registration forms for the weekend self-defense workshop.

I wasn't sure where the shooter was hiding, but it sounded as if the shots had come from near the northern shore of the lake. We'd stopped to picnic here on the eastern side, where the trail overlooked deep blue water. Needing to find out what was going on, I stayed where I was and looked up, scanning our surroundings. Ducks took off in a flapping frenzy of wings beating the glassy surface of the lake in a spray of drops. The stellar's jay that had been eyeing our picnic squawked and sailed after them. Russet-colored grasses of the meandering meadow twitched and waved where a stream emptied into the northern end of this mountain lake. Where the sound of gunshots had come from.

"Was that a gun?" Libby said, choking on her words.

Harlan shushed her and then whispered at me. "Get down, Nell!"

Usually, students should address me formally, using my surname to show respect, but since these workshop students hadn't signed contracts yet as my long-term students, they didn't know the martial arts codes. I let it pass.

It was the middle of September, a little early for hunting season. I didn't know exactly when the season started, but I was pretty sure it wasn't for a couple more weeks. The fluorescent orange and pink vests that the folks down at the ranch had made us wear over our tee shirts had just been a precaution for our hike.

Apparently, I was wrong.

It wouldn't be the first time. My teenage daughter, whom I'd left back home in Boulder for the weekend, could point out exactly how many times I'm wrong.

Dodging wild bullets wasn't supposed to be part of the curriculum for our weekend workshop retreat.

Great.

I knelt down beside my three companions. We angled ourselves to keep the rock outcropping between the lake and us. Apparently, this part of the mountains wasn't as remote as we had thought. There'd only been one vehicle at the trailhead, some kind of pickup truck parked next to the bar that blocked a fire road. The trail, which we'd followed instead of the road, took off from there, and we'd passed only a couple other groups of hikers along the way. They hadn't been wearing hunter's orange.

"This time of year," I said confidently, "it's a hunter."

Despite my show of confidence, I couldn't help but wonder what I had led my potential students into. I did not let on about my doubts, which kept cropping up like un-whacked moles.

Nor did I point out my tendency of late to stumble across dead bodies. Five of them in as many months. Sheesh.

"What if," Libby said, "it's...n-not?" Fear glittered through the brown curtain of bangs covering her eyes as she cringed closer to the rock.

"What do you mean?" Harlan said to her, his own eyes widening. The bony outline of his jaw jutted out in sharp lines, in need of a shave. The sparse bristles looked more like the prickles of a cactus rather than the beginnings of a beard. "What else could it be? You think it's a sniper?"

Libby folded into a tight ball and quivered.

Andrea punched Harlan in the arm. "That's not funny." It was a classic front punch, and it made her look like a natural for the martial arts. She was almost as short as me, and she was a real, perky fireball, besides. With proper training from me—head instructor at Callahan's Karate—I figured she could develop a wicked front punch.

"It's not supposed to be funny," he said. And I believed him. I suspected he didn't have a funny bone in his body. "Now that there are so many terrorists in the news these days."

"Do you really think terrorists would bother coming here?" I tried not to let my skepticism show.

"Why not?" he said. "You can't rule them out."

"In cities, sure. But in a place like this, you'd more likely find hunters."

Libby glanced up. "You mean, they're shooting *animals*?"

I nodded. *Uh-oh.* We were a group from left-wing Boulder, where the plains meet the Front Range four thousand feet lower in elevation than our current position. More importantly, animals rule. There are no pet-owners in Boulder. It's the city of guardians of animals, and that included wildlife.

"Then," Andrea said, "why on earth did you schedule the workshop *here*? In this place?"

"It was available," I said.

That was true. Here we were in the height of leaf season, when tourists trolled the Rocky Mountain high country for aspen gold and tied up the majority of hotel beds on valuable weekends. There hadn't been a lot of venues to choose from, due to our low funds, but I had a few chits to cash in on. Friends of friends came through for me, even though not all of the friends in the chain were all that friendly. We were lucky to have found this place. Well off the paved roads. Deep into the mountains. Far beyond the range of day hikers and casual tourists.

Not so far away for the hardier types, though, like backpackers. And hunters.

The annual show of gold, swathing the aspens with broad strokes, was supposed to sooth our souls. Heck, with my paycheck in question these days, any kind of gold was something less than a kick in the butt.

"We can't stay here next to these rocks," Harlan said, whispering. "We're sitting ducks."

"Oh, no!" Libby moaned. "What are we going to do *now*?"

"That's stupid," Andrea said. "If it's just a hunter, as Nell says, then he's not going to shoot us. He won't, will he?"

"Right," I said, appreciative of any kind of support I could get. "And no worries. He already knows we're here. He's hunting game, not us."

"How can you be sure?" Libby's voice quavered.

I wasn't. But I couldn't tell her that. I patted her shoulder. "It's okay. We're safe in our bright vests. That's why the people at the ranch made us wear them."

She didn't look convinced.

"Well, if that's all it is," Andrea said, "then someone should go talk to him and make sure he knows about us. I'll do it." She jumped up from behind the rock and charged toward a faint deer trail that traced a route through the underbrush by the lake's edge.

The deer's path would have led to its death...

"Hey!" I called. "Come back!"

She didn't.

In martial arts, hesitating means you lose the point. So I sprang to my feet.

"You guys stay here," I told Harlan and Libby. "And stay down, for goodness sake."

This was definitely not a good idea, but I had no choice. I had to go after Andrea and keep her from becoming someone's target practice.

No one shot us, so I kept going after her. That young woman was fast. She'd already disappeared from my sight.

I sprinted down the trail. Around me, aspens shimmered. The breeze not only stirred the leaves but also wafted the air with a hint of vanilla from the Ponderosas. Goosebumps tickled the back of my neck. Maybe we were running into a trap at the barrel end of a hunter's rifle.

What if the hunter was color-blind? How would he know our darting motion wasn't his prey?

"Don't shoot!" I shouted, waving my arms. "We're a group of hikers here!" I stretched up on my tippy-toes, making myself taller and bigger. It's standard advice for meeting wildlife on the trail such as bears or mountain lions, and I hoped it would work for hunters as well. If he realized we were hikers and not game, he wouldn't shoot us. Right? That was the theory.

I tried not to think about other possibilities to explain the sound of gunfire. If Libby's fears were right and it wasn't a hunter, Andrea's headlong dash could insert her into someone else's private argument. And if Harlan's theory was right, the terrorist would be zeroing in on the commotion she and I were making. A shiver crept down my spine. As distressing as those thoughts were, knowing that my students felt trapped behind the rocks, with their safety possibly at risk, disturbed me even more.

"Andrea!" I called. But I couldn't see her. Forging ahead,

I patted my jeans pocket for some form of assurance. All I had there was a very old cell phone with no bars. No signal at all. I wouldn't have known about the no bars part if not for all the selfies my gang kept pausing to take, all the way up here from the ranch where we'd recently checked in. Without bars, they'd wailed, how were they going to send photos to their social media feed?

"You're not," I'd told them. "The point of this weekend is to isolate ourselves from all the trappings of technology. For one weekend we are going to leave all those crutches behind and just connect with nature and each other. We are going to focus on awareness of our surroundings."

Oh yeah. And now we might actually *need* that connection to the rest of the world if we were going to get any help. Except we couldn't. The rational part of me still wasn't convinced that the guy on the other side of those gunshots presented a true emergency, but the mom in me worried about accidents. Someone could end up lying in the grasses, bleeding out.

Andrea.

I ran faster. A moving target, at least, was more difficult to hit.

Overhead, a jet's faint hum and its com trail reminded me just how far away other people in the form of potential help were.

Back at the ranch, there were plenty of people who knew we were out here. Willow, for instance, the driver from our carpool. She hadn't joined us on our hike because she'd pleaded an altitude headache and had retired to her room with extra bottles of water. I figured the drive had tired her, or maybe she had just wanted to wimp out of extra exercise.

I couldn't argue with biology, or physics, or whatever culprit it was that made the human body suffer at close to ten thousand feet in elevation. We were accustomed to a mile high, but not to this.

It was the same with my soon-to-be ex half-sister-in-law Gillian—Jill for short. She'd wimped out, too. But good old Jill. After some last-minute no-shows, she'd let me twist her arm to come along and round up our numbers to seven—the minimum number required by my boss.

And then there was Woody, our host at the ranch. He'd helped check us in when we arrived by car late this morning, and he'd given us a brief sketch of the grounds. We'd had to follow the driveway past the stables before finding the fire road that led to the trail that led up here to this lake.

There were others at the ranch, too, who knew we were out here, the staff who had handed out these vests. But right now, they seemed as far away as the passengers on that jet, disappearing out of sight.

I pressed on, pausing behind boulders and clumps of trees that dotted the trail and waving my arms when I moved out into the open areas of brush. Staying alert to my surroundings, I tried not to trip over loose rocks and tree roots.

I rounded a bend, and then nearly bumped into Andrea. She stood motionless in the middle of the trail with her hands planted on her hips. With her initiative, she would definitely make a good martial artist. Maybe not such a good student, since she didn't listen very well to instructions.

"Is that him?" she said, squinting at some waving, russet grasses a hundred feet or so ahead in the meadow.

"I have no idea," I said, "but we shouldn't bother any

hunter. He's not going to shoot us in our orange vests. That's why we wear them."

She snorted. "What are we supposed to do? Cower behind rocks the rest of the day? Not me."

The thudding sound of running footsteps pounded behind us, and I whirled around. Harlan's head bobbed into sight as he ran around the bend towards us. He slid on loose rocks but recovered his balance well. "Did you find him?"

"There's something over there," Andrea said, pointing at the meadow.

I peered down the trail. "Where's Libby?"

"Still hiding behind those rocks," Harlan said.

"Let's go make sure he knows we're here." Andrea charged forward.

"Hold on," I said, hurrying after her. If anyone was going to be shot at, it would have to be me. I could talk a brave talk. That didn't necessarily mean that I felt brave, but I was still responsible for this gang, even if they acted like a herd of cats. I needed to take the lead.

It occurred to me that Libby's fears might be right, and the shooter might not be a hunter. Maybe he was a maniac who lurked in the bushes, waiting for us. Maybe—

"Oh!" Andrea cried, sliding to a sudden stop before I could overtake her.

I nearly bumped into her as I fought my momentum to stop beside her. She covered her mouth and stared at an area of scrubby trees at the edge of the meadow fifty feet or so away from us.

"What's that?" she said, pointing at the movement in the underbrush.

Tiny, black heads bobbed there. Blackbirds. I crept closer.

The birds were having a convention. I was so intent on their frenzy that I almost missed the other thing. The barrel end of a rifle poked out of the grasses beneath a barberry bush. I froze.

In the next instant, I unweighted myself and side-stepped fast out of the rifle's range. The rifle lay on the ground. It did not follow my movement. There was not so much as a jerk or twitch that would indicate someone's antsy fingers holding it. My muscles relaxed. The rifle appeared to have been discarded there. I took another step closer.

Uphill, a few feet away from the rifle, the birds danced apart, revealing the object of their attention. Sprawled on the ground behind a twisted clump of cedars was a man's outstretched arm. His rifle arm. It wasn't moving.

When I saw the rest of him, lying face down, I could tell at once that he wasn't alive. I did not need to see his face to know. The thin strands of white hair across a grayed, bare scalp told me it was Woody.

Chapter Two

"Woody!" I shouted, just in case he was still alive.

He didn't respond.

Nothing moved around him, except for the birds, who retreated a few feet to watch Andrea, Harlan, and me. The grasses cushioning Woody's body lay as still as he did. There was no shuddery movement of the red crosshatch of his plaid shirt to indicate he was breathing. Where was his orange vest?

Andrea squealed and jumped back. "Is he dead?"

The birds lifted into the sky, flapping like a black shroud. I dropped to my knees beside Woody. Harlan stood over me as I reached my fingers to Woody's neck. My probings could find no pulse. His flesh felt cold, and I touched something sticky. Blood. I jerked back.

With all that blood, I was pretty sure he hadn't died from a heart attack.

I wiped my fingers in the grasses, and they scraped against something that felt like a stick. *Ewwww*. It wasn't. It was a dried bone, about the size of a finger. I dropped it as if it had stung me. I crouched there, frozen in place for several heartbeats.

It wasn't a finger bone, I realized after taking a few deep breaths to restore my reason. And even if it was, it wasn't

Woody's. His hands were intact, at least what I could see of the balled-up fists angled beside his body, looking as if he'd been punching something when he fell face first. But this thing sure looked like a finger. Kind of decayed, though. I decided then that it must be a piece of antler.

"What are we going to do?" Harlan said.

"We need to get help," I said.

"It's too late for Woody. Do you think...?"

He didn't have to say it, because all of us must've been thinking alike: the gunshots we'd heard. Woody hadn't shot himself. Someone else had shot him. We glanced over our shoulders where we'd seen grasses moving a short while ago.

Andrea pointed across the meadow. "Look!"

There was a truck.

Where the base of the mountain met the russet and ochre bowl of the meadow, a fire road carved a dirt line. It was probably the same fire road we'd crossed at the start of our trail.

The truck wasn't moving. Parked at the edge of the road, it looked like an antique pickup straight out of a Norman Rockwell painting. Either its paint had chipped off, or it was a matted shade of faded brown. It looked like one of the broken-down vehicles I'd seen back at the ranch. Wherever it came from, it was a miracle it had made it up here, over steep inclines, potholes, and rocks. No one sat inside.

Because its driver must've been Woody, and Woody was over here. Dead.

"Let's get back to Libby," I said, standing up on shaky legs. I nudged Harlan and Andrea onto the trail.

They didn't resist.

We crept single-file. I took up the rear position, inserting

22

myself between my students and whoever had shot Woody. The shooter was still out there, maybe hiding in the grasses. Was he watching us?

So much for our idyllic picnic, kicking off the start of what was meant to be a fun, three-day weekend.

Then the earth shuddered beneath my cross-trainers and vibrated up my legs. Thundering hooves hammered the ground behind us, crunching sticks and twigs. I turned in time to see a broad antler push through a thicket, snapping off branches. An enormous animal charged out of the brush.

"Moose!" I shouted, lunging at Harlan and Andrea and shoving them out of its path. I dove after them as hooves pounded closer.

We landed in a splat beside the path. Rocks scraped my knees and palms. My flesh stung. My bones jarred from the earth's hammerfist. A cloud of musky animal scent choked the air as the moose thundered past, spraying us with droplets of...

I didn't want to know what it was. I rolled my cheek up from dusty dirt in time to see something stick-like flapping from the moose's shoulder. The stick was a spot of lime green flashing by. It was an arrow, I realized, as the moose disappeared into forest.

Andrea and Harlan squirmed beside me.

"Are you all right?" I said, helping them up.

Andrea wiped a streak of dirt from her arm and gasped. "Did anyone get some pics?"

Harlan shook his head. "Do you think that's what the hunter was shooting at?"

"That moose was shot by an arrow," I said. "Not a gun."

"You think the hunter did it?" Andrea said.

Harlan brushed himself off. "Of course he did. He must've shot Woody, too."

"So where is he?" Andrea said.

If he was a real hunter, he'd still be nearby, chasing his prey. I twisted around, scanning our surroundings. Someone was out there. Either a rifleman, an archer, or both. But nothing moved anymore. Not even the breeze stirred the grasses of the meadow.

"You think he shot Woody with an arrow, too?" Andrea said. "We didn't see his chest. There could've been an arrow stuck in him."

Harlan frowned. "We heard gunshots, remember?"

We listened, but all we heard now was the sweet sound of silence. The absence of sound tamped the mountain air, smothering the lake with an eerie calm. No ducks squawked, no ground squirrels chirped. There were no distant voices of hikers. No more gunshots. That was a good thing.

"Let's keep going," I said. "Libby will be wondering about us."

We darted on, and around the next bend, an unnatural spot of color flashed at me from the shadows of the undergrowth. Lime green. The others forged ahead, but I paused to kick the color loose with the toe of my shoe. It was a small piece of plastic, maybe an inch long and spherically shaped. I'd seen it before. It was a piece of the arrow that had fallen from the moose's shoulder.

I stooped down to pick up the bit of plastic and tucked it into my jeans pocket. Then I did a three-sixty, scanning the meadow, the forest, and the lake. Everything looked peaceful. No one aimed a weapon at us. No carrion birds circled overhead, either, hinting at a hunter's nearby cache.

We continued on, following the rim of the lake, making our way back to our picnic site and Libby. She hadn't moved.

"Hurry!" we told her as we scooped up the remains of our picnic. She didn't ask any questions, but she must've picked up on our sense of urgency. Too many helping hands stuffed our gear into my pack. Things kept falling out, but eventually I managed to zip up the pack and slip the straps over my shoulders. Being a black belt, I was supposed to be the fittest of our little hiking troupe, but at forty-five, pre-menopausal, and a single mom of a teenage girl, at that moment I did not necessarily feel all that fit.

Then we plunged into the shelter of the forest, following the trail downhill.

Halfway down, we slowed our pace. My students were real troopers, but they were gasping for air. By now, I was pretty sure no one was following us. We could slow down. And besides, what was the hurry? Woody was dead.

We trekked on in numb silence. The air tasted crisp, the sky was the intense blue of a robin's egg, and gold dripped off aspens, shimmering and shaking and rustling like the sound of my mother's chiffon skirts. Inhaling the gold in the air, I felt its tingle from the inside out. Slowly, the cramps of stress that had driven us in our flight eased from my mind.

Yikes. I'd had such high hopes for this workshop. I *had* to make a go of it. This weekend was all about my livelihood. My daughter's future. Money.

The karate studio back home in Boulder was losing money faster than my boss, Mr. Callahan, could drum up funds from his money-bag investor friends. He'd informed me only a couple of weeks ago that we needed to increase our enrollment at least by twenty percent by the end of the year.

Or else.

He would have to consider shutting down the school. He didn't have to say it, but I knew what else he was thinking: thanks to me and all the trouble I'd stirred up in the form of the dead bodies I kept finding—five...now six, including Woody—people were hesitant about signing up to our school. Who could blame them?

Down in Boulder, we were a small school with only 48 students signed on, 49 if you counted my daughter Terra, who had only recently joined the white belt class, tuition free, as a perk of my job. Two more were currently in the free trial period. Twenty percent meant that we needed at least nine and a half new, paying students to sign on.

Thus, my bright idea for staging this self-defense workshop for adults. To recruit new students.

So far, I had managed to drum up six candidates from a combination of my notices on community boards and my daughter's electronic postings. I hoped to sign up all six before this weekend was over, plus four kids left at home with spouses. I couldn't let anything upset any of these potential students, especially not before I brought out the contracts. If all of them signed on, I would meet Mr. Callahan's minimum and keep my job. At least for a little while longer.

I wondered how these three were coping with today's trauma. Really, I had no idea what they would be thinking. I didn't know them. All I knew about them was contained on their workshop registration forms and the small talk some of them had made in the car on our way up here this morning.

Mostly, I'd focused on the fact that each of them had some sort of income down in Boulder, and I was hoping it would be sufficient to allow them to sign up for our martial arts program at Callahan's Karate. The forms didn't tell me much about them, but their having an income was the one thing that mattered most to me, personally, right now. These workshop students were likely candidates for helping me keep my job and my status quo, shaky as it was.

I would have to think of something else to keep the karate studio afloat, but I would do that later. Now, it was all about Woody.

My poor students, too. They were gasping seriously by now, and I called for a water break. We paused to catch our breath. The memory of my first encounter with Woody washed over me as I swigged water.

I had to admit. He hadn't been the most likable guy I'd ever crossed paths with.

We had just checked in at the main desk of the ranch house. The young woman who'd helped us led the rest of my group, along with their gear, down one of the long corridors to find their rooms. I lingered behind in the reception lounge, unable to resist checking out all the antlers. They were everywhere—over the front door, in lamps, and on the wood-paneled walls. That's when Woody Woodcock banged in from a private hallway.

I whirled around and faced the owner of the ranch. He was a short, rotund man, radiating the smell of tobacco as he moved out of the shadows and into the circle of soft light illuminating the reception desk. He wore a red plaid flannel shirt that clashed with his blustery face of pink cheeks and his pink scalp, gleaming through the thinning strands of his white hair.

"Hello, little lady." His eyes roved across my flat chest displaying this year's *Bolder Boulder* tee shirt. "Don't tell me you're our little ninja?" He threw a few sloppy upper cuts into the empty air surrounding him and wheezed.

Very funny.

I acknowledged that I was the one who would be conducting the self-defense workshop, and I thanked him for his gracious hosting, even though I figured he was just trying to make a buck, same as I was. Why would he turn down an opportunity when it landed in his lap?

"You like my little collection?" he said, nodding at the Bambi watching the back of my head.

Several responses came to mind, but I settled on the easiest one. "Interesting."

He chuckled and wheezed some more. "I've been working hard to make this place what it is today. And every lick of it is for the wife, see?"

No, I didn't see. Nothing about the ranch décor had suggested any evidence of a wife's presence. No homey touches amongst the animal trophies.

He wiped moisture from the rim of one eye. "Edna's been gone almost four years now, come spring. These heads, they're all for her, in her memory. I'm gonna get me the big one, if it's the last thing I do."

That explained the décor, but I hadn't taken him for a grieving widower. "I'm so sorry," I said, not knowing what else to say.

The big one. He had to have meant a moose. A bull moose

would be the biggest trophy of all. Somehow, he justified it for his dead wife. I didn't see the connection between a moose and his wife, but it clearly meant something to him.

Puzzling over the memory, I wondered now if there was also a connection between Woody and the injured moose that had nearly run us down. I took a few more sips of water and surveyed the vista. The scenery up here in the high country was to die for, especially in leaf season.

Literally. Woody was dead.

It had taken us about an hour to hike up there to the lake, including all of our stops along the way for water and photos. Returning, we almost halved that time. The route was mostly downhill. Besides, there was nothing like a little motivation to move us along, in spite of scant oxygen.

I smelled the horses and heard their whinnies before their corral finally came into view.

But we weren't home yet. The closer we came, the slower we moved. Libby was limping by now. All three of my potential students were probably sorry that they'd ever joined me. They wanted to put our misery behind them, or so I assumed, since they had to stop and stroke the horses.

Finding no ranch hand there who could help us, I left my gang and hurried on to the ranch house. The main ranch dwelling was a low-slung, sprawling house of logs, looking as if each wing had been added on as an afterthought, rambling in the way long words squeezed this way and that onto a scrabble board. A comfortable curl of smoke rose with a woodsy smell from the central chimney as I approached.

A dark green truck with Colorado plates parked beside the front porch, blocking the driveway. Now that I saw it, I was pretty sure it was the same truck I'd seen parked at the trailhead when we started up on our hike. No one appeared inside the cab now. No rifle mounted on the rack behind the empty seat. Good.

I scurried past and yanked open the front door, flimsy thin compared to the solid thickness of the log structure. The antlers tacked above the door rattled at me. I gulped some air and burst through the front door of the ranch into the gloomy light of the reception lounge. My chest felt as if it had been hammered. I must've been running on pure adrenaline, because I had nothing left. I was feeling like a strung out yo-yo. I had to hand it to my students, who'd powered on as far as the horse corral. But then, they were only half my age.

I plunged into the dim interior of the lobby, glowing from the fireplace and the soft light of a lamp, its shade fashioned from antlers. It sat atop the chest-high counter of a reception desk, where a man stood, on the guest side of the desk, turning pages in a large book resembling a ledger. He startled as I thudded inside.

Another voice spoke from the shadows surrounding the fireplace. "Here you are, *finally*." I recognized that husky silk drifting from one of the sofas. Jill. "What on earth kept you so long? You'll never guess who's dropped in to say hello. And look what the cook has made for us—divine cookies!"

I tried to breathe, but there wasn't enough oxygen in the air. I managed to spit out, "Got to...call 9-1-1."

The man's voice barked at me in a familiar manner. "What's the nature of your emergency?" he said.

Tingles crept down my spine. Not only was he familiar with the script of a police dispatcher but his voice also sounded vaguely familiar to me.

His chunky shape pushed away from the desk, coming closer to me. "Well, well," he said, "if it isn't Mrs. Gannon."

My blood ran cold. Only Detective Rosenquist, my nemesis from Boulder, had ever called me by Max's surname.

Chapter Three

I'd always thought that Rosenquist's obsession over his black widow theory of me was just meant to get under my skin. And it did.

Apparently he hadn't changed since I'd last seen him. For one thing, he hadn't grown any taller. I'm only five feet tall, and I've always looked eye to eye in his puffy face. He might have grown a little wider, though. The pear shape of his body was plumping out enough that its folds crept up around his neck.

"It's...Woody," I said, slipping my backpack away from the sweat on my shoulders. The bulky canvas *thunked* down onto the cheap imitation of an Oriental rug. "He's dead." I sputtered out the rest of the story, and as I did, my students trickled in, one by one, joining Jill and chiming into my story with their little cries of dismay.

"I'll take it from here," said Rosenquist, whipping out a cell phone from his vest pocket and scowling at me.

What on earth was he doing here?

Then two things dawned on me. One, the truck out front must belong to Rosenquist. And two, he was the friend of Jill's friend who'd known someone who could accommodate my workshop. How convenient was that?

For the last few weeks my sis-in-law Jill had been dating

Sean Hennesey, a detective down in Boulder and Rosenquist's former partner. I'd crossed the detectives' paths several times in relation to the five bodies I'd stumbled across in as many months.

Now there were six. I swallowed hard.

With number five, Jill had been with me, and bless her heart, she'd asked me where I'd been hiding Sean all that time. As if. Thanks to Jill, we graduated to a first-name basis with our personal detective.

If Sean hadn't felt sorry for his former partner's anger management issues, the two of them wouldn't have stayed in touch, and the rest of us wouldn't be here now.

Rosenquist gave a little snort and turned his back on me. Holding his phone up to his ear, he marched to the front door.

It shouldn't surprise me that the detective had managed to acquire a phone that actually worked. He wouldn't have tolerated anything less.

However his separation from Boulder's police force had happened, Rosenquist decided to come up here into the mountains to do some serious fishing. Maybe he thought he could boss the fish around with no consequences like he'd bossed people around in Boulder. Given his pompous reaction to my news about Woody, he must consider himself a big fish in the small pond of detective work up here in the mountains.

He was close to the last person I wanted to see.

Rosenquist had always been convinced that I had done away with my soon-to-be ex, Max Gannon, whose name I had never taken. Maybe it made more sense to him than the boring truth. Max had simply gotten tired of his life, withdrew the money from our joint account, and disappeared across the border, reportedly last seen with a couple of blondes hanging off his arms. Thus, the reduced status that had lost me my cushy suburban home. I'd landed upright on my feet in a garret apartment down in Boulder. End of story, as far as I was concerned. Except, if I wanted to improve my situation, I had to make this weekend workshop a success.

But this Boulder detective—he was an ex, too—never believed me. He was determined to mold the truth around to fit his view of reality.

Now, questions flew around me in the wake of Rosenquist's departure from the reception lounge. I could hear his boots stomping back and forth outside, across the front porch. He must be calling his contacts.

Inside, Jill took charge. She slipped the orange hunter's vest from my shoulders, folded it neatly, and then herded all of us to seats around the fireplace. I didn't mind. I was beat up enough that the velvet embrace of the couch helped soothe my overworked muscles.

Jill poured coffee from a thermos sitting on a nearby table and went on, explaining to the others about "that nice Detective Rosenquist," and how he was the one who'd found this wonderful ranch for us. He'd stopped by to say hello and see if we were comfortable here at Woody's ranch.

Weren't we lucky, Jill told us, that her boyfriend's friend was here? He was a real pro handling this unfortunate matter for us.

Lucky, right.

Jill positively sparkled when she held center stage. While I waited for my heart rate to settle, she held her audience captive. She couldn't help herself, not with her fancy private school upbringing back east and the trust fund that made money a comfortable given in her life. In spite of those handicaps, and regardless of our questionable familial relationship, she was one of the best people I knew. She'd proved herself my most loyal advocate during my recent encounters with those five bodies, and furthermore, Jill liked to spoil her only niece, who happened to be my teenaged daughter Terra. Who could complain about that, even though Jill and I had apparently been born on different planets?

Basically, she was a nymphomaniac, but I'd found her skills useful the way she could tease information out of her victims—I mean, *informants*—regarding those cases of the previous five bodies.

Did I mention how lucky we were?

As my eyes adjusted to the dim light, and as my breathing settled back to normal, I took note of the others around me. Next to me, Jill settled on the center cushion of our couch. On her other side was Harlan, our lone gentleman in the workshop. Andrea perched on the armrest. In one corner of the room, farther removed from the fireplace, Libby hunched in a single armchair. Her curled-up body language told me she hadn't recovered yet from her trauma behind her rock when gunshots interrupted our picnic.

Willow, my student with the headache, wasn't here.

Jill batted her extra-long eyelashes, compliments of her personal make-up consultant, and nudged Harlan's arm. "I say let's make Harley Poo an honorary girl, so that we can have a little girl talk."

Even in the muted light, I could see him flush. He set down his coffee mug and started to rise.

36

"Gillian," I said, lifting a warning eyebrow at her.

She ignored my message and wrapped her fingers around his wrist in a claw-like grip that any beginning martial artist could easily release from. "Aw, c'mon, honey, can't you tell, I'm just teasing?"

My voice growled. "As a reminder, we are in a tease-free zone this weekend."

Andrea piped in. "Yeah, but what if there's a killer on the loose?"

"What Jill means," I said, my voice rising to an upbeat tone, "is that we're going to learn techniques this weekend that will empower us, regardless of gender, to take care of ourselves, should the need ever arise." I carefully danced around the question Andrea had raised. Had someone killed Woody, and was he out there now, on the loose? Stalking the rest of us, maybe, because he thought we'd seen him.

We hadn't.

"Right," Jill said, taking the cue. "That's what I meant." She burst out laughing, releasing the tension that hung heavy in the air. The rest of the group laughed with her, although their laughs sounded like weak little squeaks. My students couldn't help being infected by Jill's good nature. She passed around the cookie plate, carefully declining one of the little dietary bombs for herself.

They munched for a while, and Rosenquist stomped some more on the porch.

Then the glass door into the dining room rattled and squeaked. A young woman entered the lounge. Jill leaned forward, paying close attention, scrutinizing the new arrival, who looked like a model. She was tall, with a waif-thin figure, skin-tight leather boots up to her knees, and long strands of dark hair curling around the spaghetti straps on otherwise bare shoulders. She startled as she spotted us, crashed on the couches, and gave us a puzzled look.

"Oh!" She moved like a model, too, as she swayed across the room toward us. "What's going on? It looks like you guys have been hurt." Her voice lilted, matching the swing of her hips.

Maybe we had a couple of scrapes and bruises from our recent nose-dive under the moose, but that didn't matter. "It's Woody—"

"And there was this moose!" Andrea waved her arms at the wall behind the desk, pointing out the general direction where we had been hiking.

The woman smiled, a bit condescendingly, I thought. "Yes, we have a moose population around here. You need to stay back if you encounter one of them."

I glanced at Andrea, sending her calming vibes, and then spoke to the model. "It's more than that. I'm very sorry to have to tell you this, but you see, there's been a terrible accident, and..." How to break it gently to this young woman? Who was she, and how well did she know Woody? There was no way but the direct way. "I'm afraid that Woody is dead."

"Dead?" The woman covered her mouth with her hand and stumbled backwards half a step. "But that... That's just not possible! No!" She whipped around, facing the wall, as if wanting to hide her face from us.

"I'm so sorry," I said, standing up and taking a few steps closer to her. I was ready to offer some comforting arms if she needed a hug. I went on, introducing myself and my students while her shoulder blades quivered.

She straightened her back, wiped her face, and turned around. "I'm okay, thanks." She sniffed and forced her delicate mouth into a smile. "I'm Kitty Robin. I board my horse here at Woody's ranch. Came in, looking for him. He's the guy in charge, so that makes him accountable for what goes on in the barn. But dying... That's so...*extreme*. How do you know about it?"

With help from my students, I told her about our hike, our picnic at the lake, and finding Woody's body. Harlan mentioned the gunshots, and Andrea added the moose to our tale. Kitty folded her arms tightly to her midriff and tapped one finger against her upper lip as she listened. Jill studied Kitty's boots.

When we were done, Kitty said, "It's not exactly surprising. He had it coming to him."

I tilted my head sideways. Had I heard her right? No one deserved to die before his or her time. "Well," I said, floundering for a response, "Detective Rosenquist is on the phone, calling for help." I nodded at the front door. We could hear him pacing across the front porch. "So all we can do right now is wait. Although, maybe we should go pack our things and get ready to clear out." I nodded at my gang and started toward the corridor that led to our rooms.

"Wait," Kitty said. "Where are you going? Don't you think you should talk to the sheriff? I'm sure he'll want to talk to you, that is, if Fiona will let him handle things."

"Fiona?"

"The cook."

Right, I knew that. Fiona had prepared our savory

picnic and afternoon cookies to boot. I didn't know why ranch business was up to the cook. Neither did I want us to be in the way during such a private time.

"She likes to boss everyone," Kitty said. Her voice rose, sounding desperate. "She needs someone to fuss over. Especially now, don't you see? She was his sister-in-law, and she'll go to pieces when she finds out. If you stay, it will help take her mind off all this. You've got to stay."

"Well..." I said, looking expectantly at my three students. "What do you think?"

"That's what we came here for," Harlan said.

"Self-defense," Andrea said. "And boy, do we need it now."

Libby straightened from her slump. "Let's stay."

"Whatever," Jill said.

Kitty sighed. "I should join your workshop. I could use some help along those lines, too."

I brightened inside. "We'd love to have you. We plan to start at nine tomorrow morning. That is, if we end up staying."

"You will," Kitty said. "Trust me."

"Okay." I would still have to check, and I supposed it would be with the bossy Fiona, who was also next of kin. Until I confirmed that, maybe I could make myself useful. While Rosenquist was making arrangements for Woody, I could help the other problem. That moose. I spied an old model telephone, the type that connects to a landline, sitting under the antler lamp on the reception desk.

"Do you know a local number for the wildlife department?" I asked Kitty.

"Let's see where they keep such information in all this

mess." Clicking the two-inch heels of her fancy cowgirl boots, she model-walked around to the hotelkeeper's side of the desk and rummaged around, slamming drawers, acting both familiar with the place and disgusted by its disorder. Finally, she pulled out a laminated card with telephone numbers and handed it over to me.

I found a number for a game warden, dialed, and waited for someone to answer. While I waited, Kitty retreated back across the lobby. "I'd better go prepare Fiona for the blow," she said. "She's only the cook, but she runs this monkey farm." She rattled the glass door, pulling it open, and disappeared back into the dining room.

The ringing over the phone line stopped, and a man's efficient voice spoke to me, identifying himself as Jeremiah Lester, a game conservation officer for Colorado Parks and Wildlife. Pushing the encounter with Kitty to the back of my mind for now, I identified myself and explained to him what had happened. I started by telling him about Woody, and the game warden responded with more remorse over the phone than Kitty had shown. And regret. Woody had been known to live dangerously, Lester told me, especially since his wife's death.

Then I went on to ask if there was anything we could do to help the wounded moose. We'd heard gunshots, I told Officer Lester, and later, the moose had nearly run us over. How badly had he been injured from an arrow to the shoulder? Had he run off to die somewhere? Couldn't anything be done to save the moose?

The game warden thanked me politely for calling and informed me that bow hunting and muzzleloaders were in fact legal for moose at the moment. Therefore, the archer who'd shot the moose with an arrow had been legitimate. As for the gunshots, was I sure I hadn't heard a muzzleloader instead of a rifle?

Well, no. I wasn't sure of anything.

However, Lester went on, abandoning the game was most definitely *not* legal. Nor rifles, not now.

"We appreciate all tips on suspicious behavior," Officer Lester said, "since any one of them could lead to the apprehension of poachers."

I sucked in my breath. *Poachers!*

Well, sure. I had definitely heard two shots in rapid succession, and that most likely indicated something other than a muzzleloader.

That made the shooter a poacher. Maybe he was also Woody's killer. Had Woody gotten in the way of a poacher? Which meant that my students and I had stumbled into the middle of it, too.

Chapter Four

Poachers! **My heart** hammered. My breath rasped over the phone line.

The game warden went on to tell me that he would be on his way here to the ranch shortly. It would take him approximately forty-five minutes to arrive. He had two mountain passes to cover between here and there. All things considered, I thought forty-five minutes was probably too optimistic. It was more likely to take him an hour at least.

I understood. Really, I did.

I thanked him for his time, urged him to hurry, and hung up. But I wouldn't give up.

Leaning against the reception desk, I scanned the laminated card again and found another number. It was for the veterinarian who took care of the horses that lived in the ranch stables. I dialed the number. An answering machine with a clipped, clinical message directed me through an agonizingly long menu before I could finally leave my own message for Dr. Vicky Newman. Would she even hear my questions before the moose dropped dead? It was doubtful she could do anything to save him, but maybe she could offer some advice.

Sounds of voices carried to us from outside on the front porch, and then the door flung open. A woman burst inside

43

to the reception lounge. Curls bubbled around her head, and I recognized her as Willow, the student who'd stayed behind from our hike, pleading an altitude headache.

"So you've been outside all this time?" Andrea said, popping her gum on the couch in front of the fireplace. "Where'd you go? We thought you were in your room, taking a nap."

Willow shrugged, and the grimace on her face told us it was none of our business. She pointed behind her. "That fisherman out front said Woody's been shot!" Her voice rose, sounding like an accusation, as if we'd done it ourselves.

But Andrea's question echoed my own thoughts. Willow certainly hadn't been in her room just now. I lifted my eyebrows quizzically at Jill. Since she'd also stayed behind from our hike, maybe she knew where Willow had gone. Jill avoided my glance, staring thoughtfully at the glass door where Kitty had exited.

But I was glad that Willow's headache must've gone away. I didn't know anything about her, having just met her in person that morning when we carpooled up here from Boulder. She'd been the driver, and we'd ridden in comfort in her large SUV.

"We don't know for sure what happened," I said soothingly, "but there's been a terrible accident. I'm afraid that Woody... didn't make it."

I hadn't said that Woody had been shot. We'd only assumed that's what had happened. It seemed likely with all the blood. Plus, we'd heard those gunshots. Had I told Rosenquist that? I must've told him. In the confusion of the chaos, I couldn't be sure of anything.

"And that's not all!" Andrea's high-pitched voice rose above the murmurs and gasps circulating the room. "There was this giant moose." Andrea held her cookie up high above her head, presumably to indicate size of the moose and not to show us her cookie. As tiny as she was, her stretch wasn't nearly high enough to convey the size of that bull moose. "It could've killed us, the way it charged at us."

"It must not have been hurt very bad," Harlan said. "Good thing we got away in time. Otherwise..."

A deathly pall of silence filled the air. It was dark in here, with the clutter of antiques and narrow windows. Flames flickered from the fireplace, lighting the glass eyeballs of a deer head trophy that watched us from the wood-paneled wall. Shadows danced across the somber faces of my students.

One of us could've been killed, instead.

Harlan didn't have to say the words. I could tell that's what everyone was thinking. Whoever had fired those gunshots we'd heard during our picnic had a gun. Had he lain in wait for his victim, who'd turned out to be Woody? It could have so easily been any one of us. But jabbering about the moose seemed to take my students' minds off the potential danger they'd escaped. They'd rather talk about the moose than Woody's death. It was safer.

It hadn't been safe for Woody.

Then it hit me. He hadn't been wearing a hunter's orange vest over his red plaid shirt. He and his staff had made us wear them. Why hadn't Woody followed his own advice?

"Dead?" Willow said, breaking the silence as she stormed across the room. "You're saying he's *dead*?"

The sounds of creaking vinyl rippled through the room as everyone shifted on their seats with Willow's pronouncement of the d-word, too close to a reminder of their close call. Jill jumped up from her sofa and marched across the room to my side. She leaned close and whispered in my ear, "Don't tell me this is happening *again*."

"Shhh," I whispered back.

Willow, who'd nearly collided with Jill, paused at the window overlooking the barnyard and chugged water from her shiny bottle. At least, I assumed it was water in there. She recapped her bottle, and still no one offered the confirmation of death.

"Well, then," Willow said, "he got what he was asking for." Her words fell like a bomb. She continued, explaining, in case we hadn't got it. "Human interference always turns out bad for the wildlife."

"Especially," Harlan said, "when certain humans want to hang some trophy heads on walls." He nodded at Bambi, silently watching us through glass eyes.

"That's gross." Willow paced the room, from the window to the couches and back again. "And it's cruel," she said. "Animals have more of a right to live here than we do. They were here first. If we humans have any use on this earth, it should be to protect all forms of life. Instead, we destroy it. You should join me in my cause at TAfA."

"TAfA?" Libby said.

"You only moved here recently, didn't you?" Willow said. "It's short for Take Action for Animals. We support the rights of animals, and we take action for them."

"Oh, right," Jill said. "I've donated."

I'd never heard of it, and I'd been born and bred in Boulder. Just my luck to have recruited an animal rights activist to join us at my potentially money-making workshop at a ranch that clearly leaned to the opposite side. It was Woody's rights over those of animals. Was that why he'd died?

Jill's donation didn't smooth the air that grew thick and heavy under the weight of Willow's vitriol.

"I tried to talk him out of going up there," Willow said, "but he wouldn't listen."

"Wait a minute," I said. The laminated card of phone numbers I'd been holding at the reception desk slipped from my fingertips as I tried to process what she was telling us. "Who did you talk to?"

"Woody. Around the same time you guys left to go hike up there."

"You talked to *Woody*?"

"Yeah," she said. "I texted you that he was on his way up there. With a rifle. I thought you knew."

"She never checks her phone," Jill said.

I shook my head. "I didn't have any service." Okay, maybe I would have to get that upgrade for my phone after all. "What did he say?"

"That he'd heard reports of a bull moose up at the lake, and he was going to get his biggest trophy yet. Ugh. He wouldn't listen to me."

Apparently, Woody didn't listen to anyone, not after he'd set his sights on what he wanted. This, according to Fiona, the bossy cook. I remembered what she'd told me when I met her earlier that day.

* * *

On my way to the kitchen to collect our picnic lunches, I'd had to pass through the dining room, and that's where I'd found her, balancing on a ladder. The light was just as dim in there as it was in the reception lounge. Only a trickle of daylight came in through lace-curtained windows, further filtered by the overhang of the front porch and pine trees outside. But it wasn't so dim that I couldn't spot all the trophy heads that lined up along the length of the wall. They looked down over a dozen or so wooden tables.

My indigestion rumbled.

Fiona balanced on the rungs of a ladder, which unfolded below the chins of the trophy heads. Her purple knee socks matched the hem of her purple dress, flouncing out from under a starched, white apron.

"Oh," I said, rushing over to grip the ladder and anchor it for her. "Let me help you."

"Don't worry," she said with a grunt, "I'm not going to fall. I must've done this a hundred times."

Her arms wrapped around the throat of an elk and lifted its mount from its hook, scraping the backing against the wood panel of the wall. Further along the row beside her elk, I counted two deer heads, one big horn sheep's head, and three sets of mounted antlers without a head. Two of the headless racks were either from a deer or an elk—I couldn't tell the difference.

"What are you doing?" I said.

"Readjusting these guys. How does this look?"

I squinted at the wall. Next to the elk with whom she'd been wrestling, there was a bare space with the faint outline of something that had recently hung there. "Did you want to leave that empty space?"

"I got to make room before he changes his mind again. Men," she snorted. I presumed she didn't mean the elk but was referring instead to Woody, owner of these heads. I recalled his blustery display that illustrated his opinionated self.

"What has he changed his mind about? I hope it doesn't have to do with our being here this weekend."

"No, nothing like that," she said. Holding the elk head, she crept up another rung of the ladder and lifted the trophy across to a new hook. I marveled at her agility. "Tell me if that looks even."

"Sure, it looks good. I mean, it's not crooked."

"Anyhow," she said, "Woody is tickled to death that you're here. It's been a long time since we had a big group up here. Not since Edna..."

When she didn't go on, I waited a beat and then said gently, "His wife who passed?"

She nodded. "She was my sister, too."

"Oh! I didn't realize. I'm so sorry."

"Me too. But it's been four years now since she's been gone. And I count my blessings every day, just to have a home. I had nowhere else to go back then, and Woody couldn't keep the ranch going by himself. So it all worked out in the end, even though..." She tipped her head sideways, studying the elk before her.

Even though what? "Are you thinking of moving away?" I asked, encouraging her to finish her thought.

"No, they'll have to carry me out of here in a box." She laughed, but I couldn't join in, not over something like that.

I decided to change the subject. "Woody seems quite proud of his trophies. Did he hunt all of these himself?"

"Wouldn't he wish," Fiona said with another snort. "He bagged a couple of 'em, but mostly he gets 'em from Mr. McLean, his favorite taxidermist."

"Is that what he changed his mind about? Acquiring one of these heads?"

"No," Fiona said. "He's all over the place about where these guys should go. He worked himself up into a tizzy when his favorite rack went missing a couple days ago."

"Missing? You mean, as in stolen?" I didn't see how trophies like these could be easily misplaced.

"Right-o, that's what he thinks. But he's wrong, as usual. No one in their right mind would've wanted that ratty old thing. Antlers. *Shed* antlers."

"He was telling me just a little while ago," I said, "just how valuable these trophies are."

Fiona snorted again. "Not that one. Let me tell you, no one's going to steal a rack like that. It was two, three years ago when Woody found them. Some animals had already been at them, chewing them up. But see? He didn't mind, 'cause they were from a moose. That made them special. I always told him, 'Honey, you keep on lookin' and you'll find yourself a rack in better condition.' Didn't matter what I said, 'cause he was awful proud of those ratty antlers, even the way they was."

"Then, what do you think really happened to them?" I said.

"I reckon he took it down himself to make way for the new one Mr. McLean is going to deliver later today, and he just forgot. Now I've got to change everything around, so Woody don't throw another hissy fit. Men. Who can figure 'em?"

Fiona scrambled down the ladder with a grace I hadn't

expected from someone her age. From the salt and pepper hair bundled at the nape of her neck, I was guessing she was in her late fifties and probably exercised with nothing more than kitchen utensils. Back on terra firma, she stood next to me and tipped her head up.

"Do you think I've left enough room for the new one?" she said, studying her handiwork. "He's all fired up. And what Woody wants, Woody gets. He's got his eyes set on another trophy, 'the biggest one yet,' he says. I told him to wait. Get somebody to go up there with him and help him. But does he ever listen to me? Never. There's going to be hell to pay, if he don't get that bull moose."

Hell to pay, right. Those were her words. And Woody had paid. Had Fiona guessed even back then that Woody could end up dead?

Chapter Five

I paced over to the back window of the reception lounge and leaned against its cool pane of glass. He was a stubborn man, that Woody. He hadn't listened to Fiona about waiting for help, and now he was dead.

The view through the window overlooked a rutted driveway, and opposite that was the main barn, its warped, wooden siding a weathered gray. I watched as the upper half of a Dutch door slammed open just then, and someone—a ranch hand, no doubt—moved jerkily in the shadows of the barn's vast interior.

Behind me, Willow made some growling sounds of her disapproval. "I told Woody that what he was doing was wrong. He should leave the animals alone. Animals in the wild are the original recyclers."

The lower half of the barn door opened, and a figure emerged from the shadows inside the barn. It was a woman, I could tell from the curves showing through her tight jeans. Her long curls flounced as she stormed out into the light of day. Even mad, she wiggle-walked just like Kitty Robin.

As she got closer, I saw that it *was* Kitty. She'd gone looking for Fiona, to break the news of Woody's death to her.

Oh gosh. *Poor Fiona.* She was his sister-in-law. How

was she handling the news? Someone should be with her. I decided it would be me. After all, I had to talk to her about our plans.

Leaving everyone else behind in the reception lounge, I retraced my way through the cook's domain. What would she do now without Woody? This ranch was her life. She'd made that clear. I was sure she was strong enough to handle telling the staff without our support, but I wanted her to know that we were here for her, in case she needed us.

I also wanted to find out if Kitty had been right. Should we stay, so that Fiona could "fuss" over us, or should we clear out? Only Fiona could answer that.

In the dining room, the animal heads watched me from the wall. In the kitchen, I could smell the lingering traces of freshly baked bread, but there was no Fiona. If I was quick enough to intercept cowgirl Kitty outside in the driveway, maybe she would tell me if she knew where I could find the cook.

I pushed through the back door to the sunshine of the great outdoors.

Apparently, I hadn't been quick enough. Kitty had vanished. But someone else emerged from the barn just then, following in the wake of Kitty's stormy trail. Probably the person who had caused her storm. Maybe even the person behind the complaint Kitty had wanted to file with Woody.

He was a skinny man dressed in denim coveralls and an enormous cowboy hat, wider than his shoulders. I'd not seen him before. He shook a fist in the air, yanked off his hat, and flung it to the dusty ground.

Should I approach an angry stranger?

Or should I not approach?

While I debated with myself, he must've seen me standing there in the kitchen doorway. Even from this distance, I could see his face flame scarlet. He shrugged, and then swooped down to snatch up his hat, as if his little demonstration had been some sort of rodeo act all along.

I decided to approach.

The young man dusted off the hat and doffed it at me as he replaced it atop his shaggy blond head. He scuffed the metal tips of his boots in the dirt, stirring up a small cloud of dust.

"Hello!" I said overly cheerily. I stopped short, near enough to casually converse, but far enough away from him that I remained outside his striking range. I balanced my weight evenly on the balls of my feet, ready to move fast, if necessary. I didn't know what his anger made him capable of doing.

"Hep you, ma'am?"

"I'm looking for Fiona. The cook. She's not in the kitchen. Have you seen her?"

"Can't rightly say, ma'am. She don't come 'round the horses much. Them horses are my job, not hers. You one of the guests?"

I nodded. He looked as if he couldn't be much older than my teenaged daughter, and so I relaxed my stance and stepped closer, holding out my hand. "Nell Letterly, here for the weekend workshop, although..." I bit my lower lip, wondering how soon we would have to cancel on account of Woody's death. I was betting that Fiona—or whoever was left in charge—would have other things on her mind besides fussing over unwanted guests. Sooner, rather than later, we would have to leave.

"They call me Blaze," he said, taking my hand and giving it a bone-crushing squeeze. "If you want to book a horseback ride while you're here, I can help with that." He gave my hand one last hay-baling shake, and then released it.

I smiled, or maybe grimaced, pretending to think about the possibility. Really, though, I was wondering how he'd risen so fast to this level of job responsibility.

"Are you a relative, too?" I hoped not, on account of the bad news someone was going to have to tell him, but the question spilled out of me before I could remember to restrain my curiosity, politely respecting other people's privacy.

Apparently, his pedigree was more important to him, because his chest swelled beneath the brass buckles of his coveralls. "Yep. Uncle Woody says I'm gonna take over the business one day. All I got to do is keep my nose clean and work my way up the ladder."

Oh dear. My smile faded to a frown. I didn't want to be the one to break the news to him about his uncle. That should be Fiona's job. I glanced around. Where was she?

"You want a tour of the stables?" Blaze said.

"Maybe later. But right now..." How to convey the emergency of what he needed to know and still let Fiona handle it? "Look, it's really important that I find Fiona. You must be related to her, too?"

He chuckled and scuffed the dirt around some more. "Not by blood. She and I come from opposite sides of the family. Uncle Woody took me in after my daddy—his brother—passed on. Said I was the son he never had."

That made two lonely survivors Woody had taken in: his dead brother's son and his dead wife's sister. I hadn't pegged Woody for the rescuing type. I'd misjudged him.

Heat flamed my cheeks almost as much as Blaze's had.

I couldn't keep up this charade. I was going to have to tell him myself. "Look, about your uncle—"

"Fiona never did like it much," Blaze went on, volunteering more information before I could say another word, "when her sister got hitched to a cowboy. She won't even let me step foot inside the ranch house. I got to stay out in the barn with the cats and the horses, out there where I belong. Know what? It suits me fine. But my digs next to the barn ain't on the tour." He shrugged and turned to go. "It's been awful nice talking to you, miss, but I gotta get back to the horses."

"Wait a minute," I said. "There's something you need to know. Something Fiona should tell you. But she's not here, so I guess it's up to me. See, there was this accident—"

"You mean Miss Kitty's horse? She put you up to this, didn't she?" He scowled at the driveway where the cowgirl model had disappeared, apparently heading toward her car in the parking lot out front.

"Um... not exactly. She helped me find the vet's phone number."

"Dang it!" Blaze said, sounding a lot like his uncle. "I knew it! She can't leave well enough alone. We run our stables just fine, thank you. I ask you, would we ever do anything to hurt Butterscotch?"

"Butterscotch... that's her horse?"

He snorted in what might have been an affirmative. "First off, it's her responsibility to exercise her horse herself. We only provide a stall with oats and water. The rest is up to her, but Miss Kitty is the queen of Sheba, so she expects everyone to drop everything and cater to her whims. I'll bet she made *you* call the vet for her."

He didn't like Kitty much, I figured.

"Now I get it," he said.

But did he really?

There was a breath of silence as we mused about our troubles. Just as I opened my mouth again to tell him about Woody, a buzzing sound trilled from the barn.

"I reckon I better answer that," he said, trotting away from me. He headed towards the barn.

And I reckoned I'd better keep looking for Fiona.

Blaze had been no help in that regard.

I scanned the area, shading my brow against the sinking angle of the sun. If Fiona wasn't in the barn, where else might she be? Maybe one of the sheds nearby warehoused her kitchen needs. Maybe there was a root cellar.

I strolled along the rutted track of the driveway, which curved around the back of the property, past the barn and assorted sheds, and around to the front of the ranch house. I didn't see Fiona along the way, but I did see the dark green pickup that I'd guessed belonged to Rosenquist. It still parked in front of the house, blocking the driveway, when there was plenty of room in the area designated for parking, separated from the driveway by pine trees. Only one car—my carpool's SUV—occupied the parking lot. Kitty must've taken her car and left.

Boots stomped along the floorboards of the porch. Rosenquist. It figured.

I turned to face him. "I'm looking for Fiona. Have you seen her?"

He didn't bother to answer, nor even to look up at me to acknowledge my presence. Instead, he scowled at the cell phone he palmed in his hand.

I tried again. "Is this your truck?" Even though he wasn't looking at me, I pointed to the dark green pickup splattered with pale dust.

And then, miracle of miracles. He looked up. He narrowed his eyes into little simmering nuggets, as if looking for the annoying gnat buzzing his head. Maybe it was some sort of answer.

I took it as a "yes" and headed up the steps to the porch. Leaning against the railing of the porch, I dished it back to him by ignoring him. It was an easy thing to do with that view. The Rocky Mountain high always seduced me.

From the front porch of the ranch house, I could see for miles. In the hazy purplish distance, the valley folded through a serrated skyline of mountains. I knew the main road was down there, winding through the valley, but sloping hills and pine forest obscured my view between there and here. Up here, the ranch house and its out buildings and fields spread across a gentle knoll.

Then Rosenquist startled me with his voice. A delayed response, but he was actually speaking to *me*. "As if my truck is any concern of yours, Mrs. Gannon."

I could feel my blood starting to boil, as it did every time the detective called me by Max's name. It reminded me of his long-term goal: to see me pay for whatever crime he thought I'd committed that had contributed to Max's disappearance.

This detective's persistent belief in my guilt was so unfair! But that wasn't a word in my vocabulary anymore—or at least it wasn't supposed to be—because black belts don't whine.

The distant sound of tires crunching on gravel ended this

round of our spat. I turned my back on him and listened to the whining gears pull the arriving vehicle up the last hill to the ranch house.

"Ah," said Rosenquist from behind me. "Here they come now."

A rugged 4 X 4 sprouting a bar of lights on top crested the hill and continued up the driveway toward us. It pulled off into the weeds, maneuvering around Rosenquist's pickup, and came to a stop. The designs along its white side turned the heavy-duty truck into a calling card, identifying it officially as county sheriff. Another vehicle rumbled up the hill behind this one, but it carried no identifying marks.

I sucked in my breath. It was only a question of time before the officials would want to question me.

My students and I had left a trail of footprints up there around Woody's body. Darn. How else had we inserted ourselves into a crime scene? That's what it was, I figured, considering all the blood I'd seen.

And touched.

There'd been a crime.

My mind blurred as a man who reminded me of a teddy bear lumbered out of the lead vehicle and introduced himself as Deputy Sheriff Gustafson. Rosenquist pushed past me and galloped down the steps. The deputy sheriff towered over the ex-cop as they exchanged basic information in clipped tones of voice. Then Gustafson turned to me and finally penetrated the fog of questions spinning round me.

"Nobody leave the house," he said. "We'll want to talk to all of you before we're done here."

"We assumed we would have to leave," I said.

"Wrong again," Rosenquist said.

Gustafson headed back to his heavy-duty vehicle with Rosenquist on his heels. The ex-cop trotted over to the passenger's side as if he'd done this a hundred times, riding shotgun with his buddy. Gustafson motioned to someone—an assistant, no doubt—in the unmarked truck following his. A third truck lagged farther behind in a haze of dust, too far away to determine if it had any identification on its side.

Gustafson climbed behind the wheel of his vehicle, slammed the door shut, and the procession started up. They were on their way to retrieve the body and examine the scene. Not an accident, but a crime.

Murder.

Too late, I remembered the lime green piece of plastic I'd collected, presumably from the moose's arrow, and had tucked into my pocket. I would have to hand that over, even though I hadn't thought it was part of a crime scene. In the meanwhile— and it was a big *meanwhile*—the rest of us were left behind in the ranch at loose ends, waiting until the sheriff was done with us. Then we would have to leave. I wondered if we'd ever get a refund for the lodging my boss had already paid up front? If we didn't, that should seal my fate. I'd never drawn unemployment before. Would I even qualify?

The 4-wheel official vehicles rumbled past me, heading around the house and toward the fire road. As the third truck came by, it seemed in a hurry to catch up with the others. I watched them go, three trucks making a parade.

Rosenquist was going up to the lake with the gang of investigators to "help out." I figured he was at loose ends, too. A crime scene investigation was what he'd trained for all his life. It had given his life meaning for so many years. How could mere fishing ever replace the thrill of the hunt for the criminal? And soon, when the weather turned for the season, his fishing days would be even further limited.

As long as I still had a job, I might as well make the most of it. I would gather my students and call an extra session of the workshop while we waited. It might be our only opportunity. My students might as well get something for their money before the ranch staff kicked us out. Before I had to drag home with my tail between my legs.

Chapter Six

The meeting room that Woody had reserved for us was a long, rectangular room that had been added on to one end of the barn. It had a linoleum floor, and it smelled of hay and horses, although neither hay nor horses was in sight. A thin wall separated us from the functioning barn. In one corner was a kitchenette, and folding tables stacked against one of the end walls. Half-a-dozen locked doors with room numbers—the dormitory-style rooms where Blaze and the other ranch hands were quartered—lined one long wall.

I'd rounded up my students and told them to prepare for an unscheduled session in half an hour. They all seemed eager for a distraction from the unfortunate events and trickled into our workout room, where they arranged their mats in the center of the room. Stragglers were still arriving when Andrea plopped down, cross-legged on her mat.

"So, can I just ask something first?" Andrea said with a pop of her chewing gum. "Before we get started? Why'd you ever get into karate in the first place?" She drilled me with her blue gaze. "I mean, I think it's cool and all, that someone *your* age... Oh, that doesn't sound right. What I mean is..."

Her words hung there in the air for a while and then drifted away, but I could guess what she was thinking. Her confidence in my capabilities wasn't going to improve once we got started and I laid down the no-gum law.

Libby entered just then and came to my rescue, laughing off Andrea's question. "Nell doesn't seem the type to stay home to crochet booties."

"I didn't mean *that*," Andrea said, her cheeks flushing.

I smiled, recalling the feelings of empowerment I'd gained over the years. When I started training, social pressure had belittled my role as a suburban housewife. Back then, I could do nothing right. It had been a long, uphill battle, and I still hadn't conquered all my doubts and insecurities. But I was pretty pleased with how far I'd come, baby.

"You raise a good point," I said. "What are our goals for this workshop?" I wanted to tailor the instruction to meet their needs. Hopefully, we would at least get that far; then, maybe I could resurrect this in the studio down in Boulder. With luck, some of these students would join there, anyway, and save my job. "You might not even know yourselves what your goals are for the martial arts. We'll take a little time at first, talking about them."

My students exchanged glances, which read to me that they really had no clue about a goal, neither for the workshop nor for martial arts. Or maybe they were just reluctant to talk about themselves.

I jumped to my feet, energizing my students with a show of energy that I didn't necessarily have. What was left of my energy was trying to peter away after our jaunts to and from the lake, a near miss from an injured moose, and one dead body. That would take its toll on anyone. "When everyone gets here," I said, "we're going to pair off. You're going to interview each other and then introduce your partner to the rest of us. Get yourselves a drink of water while you chat."

Giggles floated through the room as the rest of my students arrived. They all headed over to the kitchenette, talking among themselves.

"Take this time getting to know each other," I said, "and we'll get started in a few more minutes."

That settled, I slipped away from the room of chatter through a door leading into the barn. I had to find Fiona and find out what she wanted us to do before I started phoning up the last two students who planned to arrive tomorrow morning. Should they bother to come or not?

I stepped into the dim lighting of the barn. "Fiona?" I called out. I didn't know if she was in here or not, but I'd checked just about everywhere else. A thin layer of hay crackled beneath my flip-flops. The smell of alfalfa was so thick in the air that you could cut it. She didn't answer, so I called out again. "Blaze?"

A horse nickered in response, but its sound was faint and far away.

Blaze hadn't come running at the sound of official vehicles lumbering along the fire road. Those roads were used for emergency access through private property, and fire was a huge threat, always present this time of year. I hoped that Blaze's absence wasn't because he assumed there was a fire farther up the mountain, and he was in the midst of evacuating the horses. I needed to stop him before his efforts went too far.

Or maybe Kitty had returned, and she was with her horse—Butterscotch. I stepped past stacked bales of hay, onto the soft dirt padding of the floor. "Kitty?" I called.

Soft thuds and a rumble of horsey sounds competed with my calls. I blinked several times, encouraging my eyes to adjust to the muted light, filtering in through cracks between the boards and from an occasional open shutter. Dust motes danced in the beams of light, looking like ribbons piercing the dark interior. Outside, the late afternoon was clouding over, dimming the light even further that trickled inside.

My only experience with horses was with our own Cinnamon, who stayed out at Dad's place east of Boulder. I didn't know anything about horses that lived together in a stable. These horses sounded agitated, snorting and nickering and stomping their hooves so much that they almost sounded like a stampede.

Then I picked up another sound: soft, shuddering sobs. I kept going, past a cavernous space filled with hay, toward a corridor on the far side, lined with wooden bars that enclosed a dozen or so stalls. I didn't want to startle whoever was sobbing, so I tiptoed into the corridor and peered over the chest-high gates to each stall. Some of the nickering horses flicked their manes at me.

"Hello!" I called out, giving whoever was in here a heads-up about my presence.

The sobs broke off into a hiccup. One of the gates opened, and a voice called out, "Who's there?"

"It's me, Nell." I stepped closer.

"Oh, it's you," said Fiona, emerging from behind the gate. A strand of her salt and pepper hair dangled free from the net holding in her bun. She sniffed. "What is it now?"

"I've been looking all over for you."

"I usually take a break before the girl comes in to help me

start supper," she said, her voice snapping at me.

"I'm sorry to cut into your free time," I said. Did she really take her break in a horse stall? "But... I really need to talk to you."

Apparently not wanting to talk, she spun around on her heels and headed back into the stall from which she'd emerged.

I followed her in.

Inside the stall was a narrow space, free of hay. It didn't look as if any horse bunked here. Linoleum lined the floor, and a desk with a wheelie chair sat under the shuttered window at the far end.

"Wait," I said, "what is this place?" I did a three-sixty. "Is this an *office*?"

Framed photos tacked to the three-quarters wall, each one hanging at crooked angles. This was someone's hideaway, I realized, maybe Fiona's, and I had barged in. The heat of a flush rose up my neck from my lack of consideration.

"Sorry," I said, backing away. I couldn't help but notice the wooden and curving end of a weird instrument, poking out from the open flap of a cardboard box atop the desk. The object looked as if it could be a type of martial arts weapon that I wasn't familiar with.

Fiona followed my gaze to the open box. She stepped between the desk and me, blocking my view—deliberately? "Now, what's going on?"

"There's been...an emergency."

"I know," she said. "I heard the trucks come."

"It's not a fire. Look, did Kitty find you and tell you about it?"

A sob hiccuped from Fiona.

"I'm so sorry," I said. "I'm afraid Woody is..." How to be gentle? "He's dead."

I stepped closer, ready to encircle her in my arms if she needed me. But she turned away and said, "I already told you. I know."

"You mean...you know about Woody?" My brain cramped as I tried to process this. "But...how?"

"Kitty told me."

"Kitty?" I felt inadequate, echoing her words. I just didn't have any words of my own to say.

"Right. You know the one. Kitty Robin. She boards her horse with us." Fiona nodded at one of the horses watching us over the tops of their chest-high walls.

This must be Butterscotch, and she was a beauty. An auburn mane fell over the side of her chestnut face, where a spot of white traced a long, thin diamond shape that stretched from her chocolate brown eyes to her twitching nostrils. She let out a long, shuddering snort.

Then I remembered. Of course Kitty had told Fiona. She'd been on that mission to find her after she'd left us in the lobby.

"Kitty was out riding a little while ago," Fiona said, "when she found Woody's body. Galloped back down here and said there'd been an accident. That's all she told me. Asked Blaze to brush down Butterscotch for her while she went to town to get help."

I frowned, trying to make sense of what she was telling me. I couldn't. It didn't add up. Kitty had already known that Woody was dead, when we'd met her back there in the lobby. But she'd acted as if she hadn't known. Furthermore, she hadn't looked like she was in a rush to find help. "She didn't leave, did she? And anyway, she could've phoned instead of going to town." Kitty could've used the phone on the registration desk, but instead, she'd helped me use it for my calls.

Fiona shrugged. "It got her out of some work, didn't it?"

Which explained Blaze's anger, I thought. But still... That meant Blaze would've also known about his uncle's death when I spoke with him. Why hadn't he expressed something else besides anger, like maybe...shock? Remorse? None of it was making sense to me.

"Anyhow," Fiona continued, "speed wasn't going to change the outcome for Woody. And she must've got them here, 'cause I heard their trucks go by just now."

Fiona had been in here hiding, I realized. She couldn't face the reality of an investigation into Woody's death.

"My group can pack up and be gone within the hour," I said, crossing my fingers behind my back. I felt like a kid, hoping against hope that she'd let us stay.

She stiffened and lifted her chin. "Why would you do that?"

"We don't want to be a bother at a time like this."

"Ain't up to me. Besides, this is what we do. We already laid in supplies and hired on the girl. You can leave if you want, but don't expect any refund."

"Wellll...I guess we could stay, then." Good thing I hadn't called up the others to cancel their plans to arrive tomorrow. Maybe this was Fiona's way of "fussing" that Kitty had mentioned. "Thank you, and I'm sorry to be an imposition."

"Ain't no never mind," she said with a sniff, pushing past me and through the gate. "I didn't mean to."

Didn't mean to what? Hide in here? Let me see her crying? Confess that Kitty had been up there? Probably it was none of those. I was guessing that she was suffering from guilt. She'd been grateful that Woody had provided her with a home, and yet she'd disparaged him to me shortly before his death.

But before I could offer her a soothing response, she was gone, hurrying out through a side door that opened to the outdoors. Feeling that she needed some time alone to grieve, I chose not to follow her. She scuttled away.

Besides, that mysterious shape Fiona had tried to block from my view wouldn't let me go. And since she was gone...

She'd never know if I took a closer look, would she? Only the horses would know, and they weren't talking. The object had been left inside an open box, practically inviting examination. I glanced over my shoulder, but the door through which Fiona had left remained firmly closed. Swiftly, I marched back to the desk and bent close.

It was a curved contraption, too long to fit entirely inside the box. It looked like a three-dimensional cross, except it had a handle. And a sighting scope. It was a weapon, all right, but not for martial arts. It was a crossbow.

The surprise of my realization made me stagger on my feet, bumping against the desk, which released dust into the air. I sneezed, and Butterscotch answered me with a nicker from her stall behind me.

Within the contours of the crossbow lay a plastic case, from which ends of arrows spilled out into the bottom of the box. Lime green, plastic wedges decorated them instead of old-fashioned feathers. Even in the dim light of the stables, their unnatural shade of green stood out, almost shining with fluorescence. Just by looking, I could tell that they matched the piece in my jeans pocket, the one I'd collected at the scene where the moose had nearly run over us.

This bow and arrow had likely been used to shoot the moose! Did it belong to the person who used this office?

Now I wondered about all that. Fiona had been a little snippy with me—I couldn't blame her, given the way I'd barged in on her during her time of grief—but maybe it was because she wasn't supposed to be here, either. I was pretty sure this wasn't her office. Had she been snooping here, checking out the crossbow? She'd tried to keep me from noticing it.

I was also sure she hadn't shot the moose. She'd been on her own mission in the dining room, wrestling with that elk head shortly before the moose was shot.

Then there was Blaze, a junior Woody in training, who'd said quite proudly that the horses were his job. Wouldn't he need a place close to them where he could manage them with whatever paperwork necessities the boarding of horses required? I didn't know.

It made more sense that this place was set up as an office for Blaze. And if so, then the crossbow might belong to Blaze. Maybe Fiona had come here to tell him about Woody's death. But she thought it was an accident. She didn't know yet what I suspected: murder.

Searching for answers, I studied the crooked photographs tacked to the walls. Most of them showed a middle-aged woman, slightly overweight and frumpy—a lot like Fiona. Sisters? But unlike the cook, this woman was laughing in every shot, whether on horseback, or holding a guitar, or posing with groups of people in various social occasions. I was betting this was Edna,

Woody's dead wife. I could almost feel her ghost beside me. Strength radiated from her. I sensed that she was the guiding force behind ranch operations even today.

If the photographs showed Edna, then I decided that this horse-stall office must've been Woody's. Fiona had been here grieving for him.

I straightened the edges of the crooked photographs and found one more, its corner sticking out from behind a photo of Edna. I slipped it out and pulled it closer to study. It showed a woman bending low over a downed animal—a bull moose. The woman was slightly out of focus, but she looked familiar. Handwriting scrawled beneath her boots, and it read "Kirby."

Wait a minute. Now I realized. The woman looked just like Kitty Robin. Did Kitty have a sister, too, just as Edna and Fiona were sisters? Kitty's sister was named Kirby. It seemed an odd name for a woman, but these days you never knew.

I would have to ask Kitty when I saw her. But if I did, that would practically be a confession that I'd been snooping. I tucked the photos back in place, leaving their edges crooked, the way I'd found them.

With one last glance at the converted horse stall, I darted away, heading back through the gloom of the alfalfa-sweetened barn toward the meeting room. I didn't want to be late for my students.

Chapter Seven

When I opened the door from the animal's side of the barn into the community bunkhouse, the light nearly blinded me. Electric ceiling lights, along with the buzz of my students' chatter, swept away the last of my stealth. Stumbling, I stepped out of my flip-flops. Then I clapped my hands and strode with energy across the room. "Okay, everybody, let's get started. Who wants to go first?"

My four students, plus Jill just sat there, cross-legged on their mats, silently sipping water. I waggled my brow at Andrea, the fireball.

"Okay, I guess I can go," she said with a laugh. "There are three of us in our group." She set down her water bottle and poked Harlan, who sat next to her. "So this is Harlan. Isn't he just like so brave? Being the only guy here with us chicks?"

Harlan snorted, and Willow and Libby chuckled. Jill remained noncommittally aloof, as if distancing herself from her workshop-mates.

Wow. I had to keep reminding myself that these students were older than my teenager by at least a decade.

Andrea paused and then went on. "Harlan moved out here from Ohio, and he's been in Boulder a little more than a year, just like most everyone else who lives there. Except he doesn't actually *live* in town, because who can afford to? Did you know that most of the population has lived there less than a couple years? Has anyone here ever met a real native? Huh? Have you?"

Me, I thought. *I'm a native. I was born in Boulder, back in the dark ages.* Or so my daughter would point out. I kept quiet and let Andrea go on.

"He works at one of those software start-ups, y'know? They're everywhere. But it's not actually in town, either. The reason why he's up here in the mountains with us now? He used to get bullied back in Ohio, see? They beat him up at school all the time because he was skinny and awkward with two left feet and all thumbs and couldn't protect himself. Pretty uncool of anyone, don'tcha think?"

Harlan's cheeks flamed pink above the bristles dotting his jawbone. His voice mumbled so low that I had to strain to hear his words. "Yeah, well there's a lot of that going around, and it doesn't just happen to little kids. Even when you grow up, it keeps going on. There's always someone who doesn't agree with you, but it doesn't stop there. Look at all the protests going on around the world, and even here in our own country. If you're not with them, you're against them."

I frowned. "We ban politics in all our sessions. Can you tell us about your partner?"

"Okay," he said, "this is Jill Gannon."

Jill beamed back, eating up the attention.

"She's a grad student in business, down in Boulder, where she moved a couple years ago from Pennsylvania...uh, I forget where exactly."

"Gladwyne," Jill said, flicking her wrist as if it didn't

matter. I knew it did. Give her an opening, and she would go on about her background, telling us how she'd left the main-line, high society of Philadelphia for little Boulder on account of her half-brother and my soon-to-be ex, Max, who helped get her accepted into the business school.

And that tale of woe only brought to mind Kingsley, the private investigator with whom I'd had a close encounter of the romantic kind the month before. I wasn't ready for that, not yet. So he still remained undercover.

But back to Jill. She couldn't help it that she's related to Max. She may be whiny, but she's come through for me over and over. She hadn't done so well around those five dead bodies, but underneath that perfectly groomed, blonde exterior of hers, she's one tough cookie. And loyal through and through. She also can't help it that she's attracted to anyone in pants.

"Well, I'm here," Jill said, "as a favor to Nell. And anyway, my boyfriend was going to be busy this weekend."

Great. "Thanks for that," I said. *Too much information.* "Can you tell us about your partner?" My gaze rolled in the direction of bubbly Andrea, who jiggled on her mat and kept popping her gum.

Jill yawned. No harm intended. She just didn't like talking about other people. "Andrea's from California. She goes to CU because of the skiing."

A heavy pause hung in the air. I jumped in to remediate that. "What does she study, Jill?"

She shrugged.

Andrea giggled. "Like, everything. That's why I came along here. I just thought this workshop would be fun, y'know? And like you told us up at the lake," she pointed at me, "knowledge is a good thing, right? Even if you don't have to use it."

The heavy air returned with reminders of poor Woody. He hadn't known how to defend himself. If he had, maybe he would still be alive.

"Okay," I said with a long exhale, "who's next?"

I smiled expectantly at Libby, who shrank into a tighter ball. Next to her, Willow ran her fingers through the tangled mass of her curls, massaging her scalp. It apparently didn't help her headache, judging from the way her eyes winced shut and her angular jaw quivered.

Willow opened her eyes and glanced over at Libby, who tucked her knees close to her chin. "Libby's an astronomer," Willow said, "out here on a grant to search for extra-solar planets with one of the institutes down in Boulder. She wanted to come along on this workshop more for viewing stars than anything else, although she thinks that learning self-defense would be useful, since she often goes out at night by herself, to stargaze."

Blow me over with a feather. Say, for instance, an arrow's lime green, plastic feather.

Libby unfolded from her ball and swept her curtain of bangs away from her eyes. "It should be good viewing tonight," she said, "if anyone's interested in going out with me later on."

"Sure," I said, "I'd like to go. Maybe you can point out some constellations, and all that. All those stars look the same to me. But for now, what can you tell us about your partner?"

Libby brightened, straightening from her hyperactively shy slump. "Willow is from way up north in Minnesota, where there's more wildlife than people. When she moved to Colorado on account of her husband at the time—he was transferred, I think, for his job, something in software?—she started volunteering with TAfA. You know, Take Action for Animals? Now that she's divorced, she got hired on by the group. She needs to know self-defense because she is often faced with antagonism for her activities, work-related."

"And it's not just on account of my work," Willow said. "I think with all the confrontations going on in today's world, we have to know how to fight."

"Just a minute," I said, my smile fading. "We need to be clear about what self-defense is, and what it isn't. I'm not teaching anyone here this weekend how to fight, but rather, how to protect yourself."

"Right, that's what I meant," Willow said. "Protecting things. That's the same as fighting."

Wrong. But rather than tell her she was wrong—we always had to word things positively, and learning how to do that was still a work in progress for me—I said, "Fighting is beyond the scope of this workshop," and I left it at that.

"Oh good," Andrea said. "I hate fighting. My little sister? She always likes to beat me up. I want to know how to stop her without hurting her. Y'know?"

"The first line of defense," I said, "is avoidance. Avoid a situation and run. There's nothing wrong with running. But if that doesn't work, and you're caught, you need to know how to get away. Let me demonstrate a few examples to show you how to release from a hold. We'll start with an easy one. I'm going to need a partner."

I motioned to Harlan with one finger, and he stood up before me. I showed him what I wanted him to do, and he grabbed my arm with one wrenching grip. *Yowie!* His hand and arm felt more than adequately strong.

"How do you avoid this?" I said, letting the pain of his grip register on my face with a wince. "I can't move, right? What am I going to do, if say, he wants to drag me away with him?"

Harlan started to tug me away, but I easily released and stepped backwards.

The students on their mats sucked in their breaths. "How'd you do that?" they chorused.

"I know how," Jill said, beaming again. "It's through his thumb."

"That's right." I showed them the weakness of the thumb, how it can't retain a grip, and how that's the spot where a potential victim can free herself by pulling loose.

Tires crunched on gravel outside just then, and a car door nicked shut. At the sound, everyone came to attention, stiffening their backs, and swiveled around. We faced the door as footsteps scraped outside. The thin door squeaked open.

"Afternoon," said Deputy Sheriff Gustafson as he poked his round head inside. "Sorry to interrupt."

"Not a problem, Sheriff." I crossed the room to usher him inside. "Please come in. We're eager to help in any way that we can."

"Yes, ma'am," he said, his leather belt creaking as he moved. It cinched in a pear-shaped belly and strapped on equipment that swished and bumped against his khaki trousers. He followed me over to Harlan's side and stood there, facing the four others on their mats.

"I guess you already know about Woody," he said, rubbing

his brow. His purple baseball cap, which I did not think was part of his standard uniform, tipped back, revealing a receding hairline. "That don't make this any easier. My team is still up there, removing the body and going over everything with a fine-tooth comb, trying to come up with answers as to what in blazes went on up there. It's too early to tell just yet, but it looks like a tragic accident. It's no secret around here that Woody was just a bit obsessive about moose, in general, and now it looks like he got too close to one of them."

Gasps chorused around the room. An *accident*?

"We were just wrapping up in here," I said. We were definitely done now.

"Wait a minute," said Andrea with a gulp, as if she'd swallowed her gum, "are you saying that moose we saw up there *killed* him?"

"Well, ma'am," Gustafson said, "we can't rightly say, but it looks like something trampled him. And we know that moose are in the area. Are you the one who reported the moose sighting?"

Andrea shook her head and looked at me. "Not me. It was *her*." She pointed her finger at me.

Gustafson tottered around to study me. His head nodded ever so slightly.

"That would explain that piece of antler we found," I said. "It was next to Woody's body. Maybe it broke off from that moose when it trampled him."

Before the deputy sheriff could comment, Harlan piped in.

"What about the gunshots we heard?" Harlan asked. "Didn't anyone tell you about them?"

"We all thought Woody got shot," Andrea said. "All the blood. Wasn't he shot?"

Gustafson's round face flattened, his mouth making a straight line, his jawbone clamping into two sharp angles. He let out a long sigh between clenched teeth, and I hoped it released enough tension to keep him from popping a blood vessel. He apparently knew something that he wasn't sharing with us, and it strained him to keep that information bottled up inside. I could guess what it was. Murder. Not an accident.

Good grief. Why was he not being forthright with us?

Maybe it had something to do with that piece of green plastic I'd found and just now remembered. I dug into my jeans pocket and pulled it out. "I found this up there," I said, holding up the little wedge of lime green. "It's the same color as that arrow we saw sticking out of the moose, so I didn't think it had anything to do with Woody's accident. But now I'm wondering if maybe Woody found the moose already down. Maybe he was trying to pull the arrow out when the moose managed to get up."

"Yeah," Andrea said with a little sigh. "I bet that's what happened. Then the moose trampled Woody and ran away. It nearly ran over us." She turned to Gustafson and added, "You're right. It was an accident."

Gustafson shook his head and opened his mouth, but Harlan cut him off.

"What about the gunshots?" Harlan said.

"Woody had a rifle, too," I said.

"Okay, hold on, everybody," said Gustafson. He rummaged into a pocket, pulled out a plastic bag, and held it out to me. "Just drop that bit of evidence in here, would you, ma'am?"

"It's evidence?" Jill said with a screech.

"Of course it is," Libby said. "And it's already contaminated."

"But it was an accident." Jill jumped to her feet and faced Gustafson head-on. "Tell me that's all it was. Why do you need 'evidence,' if it was just an accident? That's what you said it was."

Gustafson sealed the bag with the green plastic inside and took a step backwards, away from Jill and her rising hysteria.

She followed him. "What are you going to do? Arrest the moose? For murder? For pity's sake!" She peered around his shoulder, throwing an exasperated glance at me, as if it was my fault. I seemed to attract crime, and Jill didn't like it.

Gustafson took another step backwards. "Ma'am, what I'm going to have to do right now is talk to each and every one of you. Find out what you might've seen. Even if you think it's not important, I got to hear it, okay?"

"Over a *moose*?" Andrea said. "Are you serious?"

"It's more than that," Harlan said. "There were gunshots, too. So he must have lots of questions."

"You'll probably want to start with me," Willow said, hauling herself up to a standing position. She rubbed her head and winced, as if still in pain. "I went up there with him."

"You went with *Woody*?" I said. "But you said you only talked to him. Out back. And then you went to your room."

"Yeah," Andrea said. "What's up with all that?"

"It wasn't my fault Nell didn't read her text messages," Willow told the deputy sheriff while nodding at me. "Woody wasn't going to wait around for me to finish what I had to say to him, so I jumped into his truck with him. I had to. I thought that maybe on the way up there I could talk him out of going for those antlers."

"Then what happened once you got up there?" I said.

"Just a minute," Gustafson said. "Don't say another word. Not any of you. Not one dang word. Not until after I've had a chance to talk to all of you myself, one at a time." He looked at me. "You're in charge of this gig, right? So I'm counting on you to make sure that no one talks about any of this matter while I escort this young lady outside." He looked at Willow.

I gulped and nodded.

"Am I under arrest?" Willow said.

"No, ma'am," Gustafson said. "Please come with me." He led her toward the door, ushered her through it, and closed it behind them.

Chapter Eight

My students dashed to the nearest window of our workout room, which overlooked the driveway between this barn add-on and the ranch house. Jill followed in her usual curious-but-above-all-that manner. I hung back in the empty center of the room.

"He's putting her in his car," one of the three said at the window. They pressed together, bobbing for a better view through the dusty pane.

Shrill squeals came from the window.

Andrea's bubbly voice floated out from the crowd that bunched there. "Oh. My. God. He *is* arresting her."

"No he isn't," Libby said. "That's not possible, not for an accident."

"Maybe not yet," Harlan said, "but just wait."

"Nell." Jill turned around and drilled me with her jade gaze. "Tell me this isn't happening. Not again." She'd been hanging around me too much of late.

"He lied to us," Andrea said. "This shouldn't happen."

He was separating the witnesses, I realized. As an investigator would do if there had been a crime. But why would he tell us it was an accident if he really thought it was a crime?

"Yep," Harlan said. "They're going to arrest her, all right."

Not if I could help it. "Uh-uh," I said. No student of mine, not even a temporary workshop student, would be falsely accused. Nope. Not on my watch.

"Nell," Jill said, "no." She flounced away from the group at the window and pounced on me, poking me in the arm when I didn't respond to her. "I know what you're thinking. Don't do it. Don't get involved. Just don't."

Willow was my student. My responsibility. I would protect her at all costs.

I only hoped she wasn't really guilty.

"I don't like what you're thinking," Jill said.

Good thing she knew, because I sure didn't. I felt a little unbalanced, wavering on my feet. It wouldn't do to let these potential students glimpse my uncertainties. Thankfully, no one noticed. They weren't watching me because they huddled in a tight ball against the window, watching the proceedings outside.

They murmured among themselves, echoing my thoughts.

Could Willow have done it?

No way. I shook myself as a reminder. Sure, Willow might've appeared angry enough to commit murder, but no matter how she came across, her agenda was to save animals. Someone like that couldn't hurt any creature, and that included humans. I bet she couldn't kill insects, either. She probably relocated box elder bugs, too.

Still...

Gustafson was just doing his job. He was probably finding out right now whatever Willow's dynamite reason had been for having been the last person to see Woody alive. I was sure there was a good explanation. We just didn't know yet what it was. Meanwhile, I had my job to do, too.

"Okay, people," I said, clapping my hands to get their attention. "You need to come away from there and stop talking to each other, as the sheriff instructed us."

The three of them at the window grumbled, but they fell away and turned around to look at me expectantly.

"What's going to happen now?" Libby asked.

"We have to wait," I said. "The sheriff wants to question each of us."

Andrea popped her gum. "I'm going back to my room. You can tell him that's where I am when he's ready to talk to me."

Murmurs of agreement rippled between the other two as their group broke further apart.

"That's probably best for all of you," I said. He hadn't specified that we all wait here, and as long as they were in a group, they wouldn't stop talking, speculating, comparing notes. I was neither a deputy nor their nursery school teacher. So I didn't stop them as they retrieved their mats and stacked them up in a pile against the wall.

"Remember," I told them, "no talking amongst yourselves. We'll meet again in about an hour and a half for dinner." I was trying to remain upbeat.

They drifted away, all except for Jill. The meeting room felt like a vacuum around us.

"We'd better ask Fiona," I said to Jill after the others had left, "what we can do to help out."

"Someone must know where she is. Maybe that 'Blaze' fellow you mentioned?" Jill tried to look both hopeful and innocent at the mention of the interesting-and-probably-handsome ranch hand's name, but she didn't fool me. "Is that what you said his name was?"

I nodded. "Do me a favor? Go look in the kitchen for her? I'd better stay here and wait for the sheriff. No doubt he'll want to talk to me next."

Jill's eager face fell. She let out a disappointed sigh. But good old Jill nodded and turned away, heading outside, leaving me alone in an empty meeting room.

Might as well make use of my time. I launched into a quick set of jumping jacks and then sank to the floor to stretch out my legs. It felt good after all that hiking and running I'd done earlier.

Funny, I hadn't noticed before, when the place had been filled with other people, but now I heard tiny sounds. Either the barn was settling or the wind was picking up outside.

Boards creaked. But that wasn't wind. It was low, murmuring voices. Someone was walking through the barn. Maybe more than one someone. Why not? The ranch hands still had their jobs to do. They moved around in the background, keeping the ranch running, in spite of the tragic circumstances surrounding them.

Maybe one of them was Blaze. He would want to know that the sheriff was here. It wouldn't take me long to find him.

I sprang to my feet and tiptoed over to the door I'd used before, the one leading into the barn. Leaning my ear against it, I decided that the voices were definitely coming from in there. And they were fading. I hurried across the hay arcade.

When I reached the stables, I saw the last person I was expecting. Detective Rosenquist. He looked out of place here, even dressed casually in hiking boots, khaki trousers, and a flannel shirt under a quilted camouflage vest. He was standing as tall as he could, peering over the chest-high gate that closed off the stall that had been converted into an office. As if he was looking for something.

His back was turned toward a woman who knelt before Butterscotch. With a competent air about her, she stroked and prodded the horse's left foreleg. A satchel of instruments sat beside her, and I guessed she was the vet. Oops. I hadn't followed through with a cancellation message.

I stepped into the corridor between horse stalls and tried to sound casual. "Why, hello, there. Back from the lake already? Have you by chance seen Blaze?"

Rosenquist spun around from his scrutiny of the horse-stall office and scowled at me. The vet paused her examination of Butterscotch long enough to mutter about the terrible tragedy of Woody's accident.

Rosenquist shook his head. "Gustafson dropped me off, and there wasn't anyone else around. I was just about to head out when Doc Newman showed up. I had to bring her back here myself."

That didn't sound like the Rosenquist I'd known. He'd never been helpful before. Nor had he ever bothered to explain his actions, at least not to me. The magic of mountain air must've reformed him from his days with the police force. Who knew?

"No problem," Dr. Newman said in a friendly voice. She didn't sound concerned at all. "I know my way around here. And particularly around this girl." She rose and stroked the white diamond shape that streaked down Butterscotch's face.

Then she turned to smile at Rosenquist. "But I appreciate your help, detective."

Detective? I wanted to point out that he and the police department had gone their separate ways, which made him no longer a detective, no longer my nemesis, no longer a potential threat to my freedom.

Steady, Nell. I was about to hyperventilate, here in this lowered oxygen. I took slow, calming breaths.

Better, I stuck out my hand. "Hi, I'm Nell Letterly, the person who left the message for you on your answering machine. I'm sorry if it was confusing, but thank you for coming. It's too late for the moose. I meant to call back—"

"Moose?" the vet said, returning my handshake. "What moose? I came for Butterscotch. Kitty called me. She said she'd meet me here, but I haven't seen her, either. Of course, everything is in such a turmoil, considering..."

Woody's death. Maybe Kitty and Blaze had disappeared together. Would the tragic events help bring them together and resolve their argument? The shirking of duties seemed inconsequential now.

Dr. Newman unwound the stethoscope from around her neck and went on. "She said something about an injury to her horse's forelegs. Best I can tell, it looks like Butterscotch has been playing too hard. She's going to be fine with a little rest."

Yes, definitely too hard. Running too hard. She'd been running away from the scene of Woody's death. Murder. Not just an accident, as Gustafson was trying to make us believe.

Dr. Newman replaced her instruments in her satchel and said, "Now, what's this about a moose?"

Once again, I related my adventure at the lake, punctuated

by a few snorts of Rosenquist's disdainful opinion.

"But," I told him, refuting his challenge to my story, "moose aren't uncommon in this area."

Rosenquist smiled with the smug grin I knew so well, and then he started to explain, again, so uncharacteristic of him. What was up with him? "I was fishing downstream from there," he said, "but the fish weren't biting, so I decided to move to another spot. But when I went back for my truck, it was gone."

I had seen the antique truck, probably Woody's, but I hadn't seen Rosenquist's truck up there. "Gone? Someone took it?"

"Gone, as in some jerk stole it."

"But it was parked in front of the ranch house," I said. "I saw it there."

"Because he didn't get very far. I started to hike down, and along the way, I found my truck, where that idiot had abandoned it." Rosenquist chuckled. "He didn't have a key to the gate, which keeps the riff-raff off the fire road."

"And you do?" I said.

Rosenquist patted one zippered pocket of his vest. "It came with the cabin Woody rented to me."

"Let me see if I understand this," I said with a frown. "Your car thief hiked up there to the lake to steal your truck, but couldn't make his escape because he didn't have a key to the gate?" How stupid was that?

Rosenquist flashed his smug grin again. "No, he hiked up there to get a jump on hunting season. Thought maybe no one would notice. When someone did—you—then, my truck became collateral damage."

My fault his truck was stolen? Then I realized he was

talking about poachers. The game warden had been concerned about them, too. "You think it was a poacher?"

"I don't think. I know it was."

"But wouldn't a poacher have his own truck?" I asked. "How was he planning on getting his quarry back down?"

"He wanted my rig."

"And he knew your truck would be there? It sounds as if he's familiar with this area."

"It sure seems that way," Dr. Newman said, jumping in to our dialogue as she snapped her satchel shut.

"I'm closing in on him, tracking his campsites, not that it's any of your concern, Mrs. Gannon." Rosenquist dug his thumbs into the belt loops of his trousers and yanked them up a notch. "There's been an uptick in poaching in this area in the last couple of years. CPW thinks there's an organized ring operating locally. They want to break it up, so they asked me to poke around a bit. Undercover, you understand."

Colorado Parks and Wildlife. Game Warden Lester had known about Rosenquist. And apparently, so did the vet, since she knew him as a detective. And how many others knew about the arrangement? He hadn't succeeded at the undercover part very well.

"And Woody cooperated," I said, "by offering a cabin to you?"

Rosenquist nodded, and I went on. "Well, it's a good thing you're on this case," I said with just a touch of sarcasm to my voice.

"Indeed," Dr. Newman said with a long sigh. "Our beautiful animals are disappearing way too fast, thanks to poachers. Jerry Lester is trying to crack down on them before it's too late. You probably encountered one of them up there. That's why it's so important to get a good description of who you might've seen. Are you sure you didn't see anyone?"

I shook my head.

"We don't know who the poachers are," Dr. Newman said, "but they do seem familiar with this area. Someone must know something, but no one's talking."

If Woody had known, he certainly wasn't talking now.

My mind leapt onward, faster than I could form the words. "So, you're suggesting," I said slowly, "that whoever fired those gunshots was your poacher. The game warden told me that rifles aren't legal now, but a poacher wouldn't care about that, right?"

"What gunshots?" Rosenquist bit off his words again.

"I told you about them," I said. Like a hundred times. Why didn't he ever listen to me? "Didn't you hear the gunshots when you were up there fishing this afternoon?"

"There are some falls upstream from where I was," he said. "I couldn't hear much else besides the rush of water. Anyway, what you probably heard was my truck backfiring when our guy jump-started it."

"I know those falls," the vet said.

I was pretty sure the sounds I'd heard were gunshots, but I let the aggravation of Rosenquist's skepticism pass. And anyway, if he was after a poacher, then why did he doubt my report? "You didn't hear anything else? See anyone?"

"Just the horse."

"What horse?"

"This horse." He pointed at Butterscotch. "Kitty's. She was riding it."

Chapter Nine

The detective gave me his smug "gotcha" grin as he escorted the vet out of the barn, leaving me there alone with the horse in question.

I patted Butterscotch on her velvety nose and leaned close, inhaling her musky scents. "Of course you were up there," I whispered softly to her. Fiona had said that Kitty and Butterscotch had found Woody's body, probably before I did. "He doesn't need to act so high and mighty with me. But I sure wish you could talk and tell me what you know."

The horse wiggled her nostrils and flicked her tail. I wondered how long Kitty and her horse had been up there. Long enough that she'd seen the whole thing?

Kitty knew what happened to Woody. If he'd somehow gotten in the way of the poacher, and if there'd been an argument, then Kitty might've seen the poacher kill Woody. She could identify the killer.

That would explain why she'd left so quickly.

Fear.

Kitty knew. Rosenquist should talk to her. Did he know that? I turned to call after him, but he was gone already.

I let him do what he had to do. In the meanwhile, I needed to think about my students. See how Willow was doing.

Deputy Sheriff Gustafson was surely done interviewing her by now. He would probably want to talk to me next. I made my way back through the barn to the meeting room.

It was still empty.

I crossed the room to the window where my students had huddled not so long ago, watching Gustafson escort Willow to his car.

The car sat empty, too. Neither the deputy sheriff nor my student was in sight.

They must've gone back to the ranch house. Feeling late to the party, I dashed outside into the waning light of that crossover time from late afternoon to early evening. The slight nip in the air reminded me that we were also rapidly losing the last glow of summer. We were crossing over into autumn, which meant that winter's blast could hit us any day now, regardless of what the calendar told us the season was supposed to be.

Gustafson stood on the porch, leaning against one of the columns as he fingered a phone. "Ah, there you are," he said, looking up, as if I was the one who'd been missing.

I jumped straight to my point. "What do you think happened up there? I really need to know, for the sake of my students. It wasn't just a horrible accident, was it? Woody getting trampled by that moose. There's more to it than that, isn't there?"

What I really wanted to know was whether or not Willow had been arrested for Woody's murder. But since I didn't want to put any suggestions into the sheriff's head, I kept mum about those specific worries.

He sighed and pushed his purple cap back, off his forehead. "We're going to find out, ma'am. Now, why don't you have a seat." He motioned to the Adirondack chairs on the porch. "And tell me everything you saw. And heard. Don't leave anything out."

I sat down and recounted once again the sequence of events: the hike with three of my students, our picnic, the sound of gunshots—

"How many?" His words snapped at me, interrupting my tale.

I thought back, rewinding it in my mind, hearing once again those sharp cracks splitting the air. "Two."

"You sure about that?" He was confusing me. Why would he question my memory about that?

"You think one of them was an echo?" I said.

"I don't know what you heard. You're telling me, remember? How many is important, and I want you to be sure. If you heard one shot, then it was probably a muzzleloader. That's legal now."

"It was more than one."

He went on. "And if it was three shots, it would've meant a hunter in distress."

"It wasn't three," I said. My blood chilled just a bit. He didn't tell me what two shots in more or less rapid succession meant, but I could guess. It was the sound of an illegal rifle. A poacher. Who might very well also be Woody's killer.

I looked him in the eye, and I could tell from the way his gaze locked onto mine that that's what he was thinking, too, despite his song and dance about a tragic accident of being trampled by a moose. Why would he hide the truth of what he thought?

"You think there was a poacher up there, don't you?" I said.

His jaw muscles worked. "I'm just collecting the facts, ma'am."

I swallowed hard and continued my report about what I'd seen and heard—finding Woody's body, the broken-off antler, the close encounter with the moose that flashed a green arrow like the piece I later found, and finally, our return to the ranch.

Gustafson listened patiently, with no further interruptions, except for scribbling a few notes in his weathered notepad, which looked chewed up enough to be a castoff from one of his kids. I wondered if he had kids.

I wondered why he'd collected that piece of arrow I'd found as evidence.

"Do you think that arrow has something to do with Woody's 'accident'?" I curled my fingers around the word. If it was an accident, why was he treating this like a crime?

Instead of answering, he fumbled inside a large shopping bag sitting on the floor of the porch. Then he produced Willow's first aid kit, wrapped in a plastic bag, and said, "Ever see this before?"

Oh darn. Just because it was Willow's didn't make her a suspect. But it might not help her case. She'd loaned it to us to take on our hike.

"Yes," I said, my heart leaping into my throat. "It's... mine." My responsibility, that is.

"How did you end up with it at the lake?"

Did he know it was Willow's? Willow must've told him it was hers. When he interviewed her in his car. Separating the witnesses. Huh.

I took a deep breath and said, "I was carrying it in my backpack. You can never be too careful in the mountains, you know. In all the confusion of gathering up our gear, we must've dropped it up there."

Gustafson scratched his head, pushing his baseball cap farther back. I could tell he didn't believe me. "Are you sure about that?"

"Of course I'm sure." He was driving at something, I could tell.

"Anything else you want to add to that?"

"Yes. What about that piece of antler I told you about? The one we found next to Woody. Did you find it?"

Maybe it had been planted there by the killer. Maybe the killer wanted to incriminate a poor moose.

Gustafson's eyebrows lifted, as if he could read my thoughts. He rolled his shoulders and massaged the back of his neck.

"Did you find it?" I asked again when he didn't respond.

"There was a bit of antler embedded in his chest wounds," he said with a sigh.

I ducked my head and closed my eyes, not wanting to visualize such a sight.

"Okay," he said in a softer tone, "I thank you for your help, Ms. Letterly. We may need to talk to you again, so it would be very helpful if you stayed in the area."

I rose from my chair. "We'll be here through the weekend, although I'm not so sure we should impose on the family at a time like this."

Gustafson nodded. "I've spoken with the folks here about that, and they want to see this business wrapped up. Woody was always going after moose. We told him time and again to leave 'em alone, but he just wouldn't listen, on account of what happened to Edna. His wife. She died in an accident when a moose ran into her car. He's been looking for that moose ever since."

"So, you're saying that he finally found the moose?" Or rather, it found him.

"Sure looks that way. Ironic." He shook his head and sniffed as he thumbed through pages of his notebook. "Now if you don't mind, miss, would you please send out the next witness? Name of Libby. She's the last one I got to talk to for now."

"She wasn't with us when we found Woody's body, so you won't learn anything from her. But what about Kitty? Have you already talked to her? Did you tell Detective Rosenquist? He needs to talk to her, too, but we can't find her. We've been looking all over for her. Where is she?"

Gustafson looked up from his notebook and frowned. "Kitty?"

"Yes, Kitty Robin. She boards her horse—"

"I know who Kitty is. Why does he need to talk to her?"

I started to explain. "Because the vet was just here—"

"I know that, too. I watched Doc Newman leave." His voice sounded squirrelly with irritation. "She was treating the horses like she usually does."

"Treating Kitty's horse," I said fast before he could cut me off again. "Fiona told me that Kitty rode her horse up there to the lake, and that she found Woody's body. That was before I got there."

Gustafson frowned at the horizon. His lips moved, but no sound came out.

"When you arrived so quickly," I went on, "I thought

Kitty had called in the report. That's what Fiona told me, later."

"See here, miss." He whirled around so fast that his cap slipped off his head, exposing a bald crown. "You leave the questions to me, understand?"

"Sure, but—"

"No buts about it. You don't know what you're getting into. It's a nasty business, and it ain't fit for a woman. Go on, now, and send out Libby so's I can get done here and go home to my supper."

My skin prickled and my spine stiffened as I backed away from him.

"And if I catch you sleuthing where your nose don't belong," he said as I turned to go, "I'm gonna have to hold you for obstruction of justice."

In a pig's eye.

I shoved the door out of my way and stomped into the reception lounge. He was a deputy sheriff, I reminded myself. Appointed, probably as a favor somewhere along a political chain, without necessarily having had any investigative experience. That's why he'd made the mistake of letting Dr. Newman go without quizzing her himself, without finding out that Kitty held all the answers he was seeking. He'd messed up, and he knew it. He was taking his irritation out on me.

But it confirmed my suspicion: murder. I just didn't understand why he was trying to make us believe it was an accident. What was he trying to cover up? And why? Willow probably knew. She was the last person to speak to Woody.

The sounds of clinking glassware floated through the open glass doors to the dining room. The staff was setting up for dinner, reminding me of the powerful mountain air appetite

I'd built up. The fire crackled in the hearth before me, and Libby sat alone, sinking down in the middle of a sofa. She sat up as I entered.

"Is he ready for me now?" she said.

I nodded.

She stood and slinked toward the door. "I don't know anything to tell him. He made each of us stay in our rooms until after we talked to him. I suppose it's okay now if you want to call the others out of their rooms. They're serving dinner soon."

And after dinner I would coax the truth from Willow.

Chapter Ten

In the dining room, the servers had pushed a couple of the smaller, wooden tables together so that our party of six could sit in one long string. No other diners occupied the few other tables that were set with mason jars for glasses and bundles of silverware rolled up in cloth napkins. If there had been any other guests at the ranch, they were apparently gone now. Woody's death must've chased them away.

We were a subdued group as we trickled in...three, four, five of us, gathering around our table. Only the trophy heads watched us from the walls as we jockeyed for position. I maneuvered toward the middle, so that I could talk to people at either end of the table.

Everyone was here except for Willow, who would've made six. We decided not to wait for her.

Harlan pulled his chair out, scraping it across the wood floor, and sat down. "Okay, who's hungry?"

Andrea, Libby, Jill, and I found our seats, keeping our conversation to low murmurs. I was probably not alone in wondering about Willow and what she'd told Gustafson. He'd seemed suspicious of her, the way he'd separated her from the rest of us. I would bet anything he knew that first aid kit was really hers. We'd borrowed it for our hike, since the one I traveled with was in my car, down in Boulder.

And why had she been acting so coy with us, only revealing slivers of what she knew, one piece at a time? What was she hiding? Whatever it was, I hoped it didn't have to do with this business of Woody's death. I presumed any student of mine was innocent, but then, I hardly knew her.

Movement at the doorway pulled everyone's attention expectantly that way. Detective Rosenquist appeared there, surveying the room as if looking for someone. Back in the barn, he'd seemed anxious to leave.

Apparently not so much. He strode into the room and dragged a chair from a neighboring table over to the head of ours. A tall, thin man in a uniform of khaki and badges trailed along behind him.

"Won't you join us?" I said, fighting my disappointment. "We have room at our table."

"Don't mind if we do," Rosenquist said. "Meet Jerry Lester. I believe you spoke to him on the phone."

The game warden. "Thank you for coming." I sprang up from my chair to shake Officer Lester's hand. He had a firm grip and callused palms. Working hands. I liked him.

But Jill liked him more. She claimed the chair next to his. "Did you find that poor moose?"

"No ma'am." His long face sagged.

"I hope it's not been a wild goose chase for you," I said, "coming all this way. Two mountain passes, right?"

He shrugged. "It's my job. Anyway, Fiona cooks up the best venison this side of the divide. It never tastes gamey when she's done. I can't miss out on that treat."

I returned to my middle seat, and Libby stood. "I'm just

going to go check on Willow," she said. "She won't want to nap through dinner."

The rest of us fell silent again, but this time it wasn't from the pall hanging over us. The server appeared with a tray of salads. At first I thought it was Blaze, then I realized he was a she, with the same slim build and blonde hair shaved close to the back of her neck. That's where the similarity ended. Heavy bangs framed thick, black eyeliner, and she dressed in tight jeans and a Broncos tee shirt.

"I'm Lillianne," the server said, passing around the salads. The number of plates she had brought out didn't serve all of us, now that our numbers had expanded.

One corner of a tattoo peeked above her collar, and Jill leaned close, studying it.

Lillianne giggled at Jill's attention and pulled her collar low enough to reveal an inked butterfly. "I'll be taking care of you tonight. We're a little short-handed in the kitchen, I'm sure you understand."

"Maybe we can help?" I said.

Harlan sprang up from his chair. "Sure, I'll help. I used to wait tables back in Ohio."

"Hey, not without me," Andrea said, jumping to her feet. They headed across the dining room.

"Thanks, guys," Lillianne called after them as they disappeared through the kitchen door. Then she turned back to the rest of us. "You're the workshop people, right? I was so excited to hear about your workshop coming here. I've always wanted to learn that kind of stuff, y'know? We don't usually have groups like that here...or complications, either."

Like the death of the boss.

"You're welcome to join us tomorrow," I said. "We'll start at nine."

Her face flushed. "Oh, I don't know. I just couldn't. My dad told me... Oh, never mind. He just thinks I don't need to know any of that stuff." She counted our heads and promised to return with more salad.

"Just a minute, honey," Rosenquist said, sticking his index finger in the air as Lillianne turned to go. "I got a message for your daddy."

Her back stiffened for the briefest of moments as she held the tray in front of her like a shield. "I'm sorry, but he doesn't live up here on the ridge."

"I know where he lives." Rosenquist's thick torso shook as he chuckled to himself. "You just tell your daddy for me that I appreciate the referral, and I want to thank him. In person. Got that?"

She rolled her eyes and said, "Sure." She marched away, faster than she'd entered.

I turned to Rosenquist. "Do you know her father from your days on the police force?" Yup. Nosy and direct, that's me.

"As if it's any of your concern, Mrs. Gannon," he said, needling me.

"Yeah, Nell," Jill said.

"It *is* my concern," I said. "Maybe you know why her dad won't let her learn a little self-defense?"

"Do you want to hire me to find out?"

It was another jab. He knew I didn't have extra money for anything like that.

Lester snorted. "You can take the cop out of the police, but you'll never take the police out of the cop."

"Won't you tell us more, honey?" Jill batted her eyelashes, fluttering them back and forth between the two men.

Rosenquist's chest swelled. "Well, okay, in fact I did know McLean back then, before I resigned from the force. He did a little favor for me, and in return..."

When he didn't continue, the game warden smiled at Jill and explained. "It's no secret. McLean introduced Detective Rosenquist to me when I was looking for someone to investigate this matter of poaching."

"And he hooked me up with Woody," Rosenquist said.

I followed their conversation like a tennis match. "I take it this McLean you're talking about is our waitress's father?"

Officer Lester nodded. "He's the taxidermist." He swept his arm around the room, indicating the animal heads and antlers on the wall. "McLean did Woody's trophy work, and in return, Woody gave his daughter a job here at the ranch."

Jill winked at me as the men admired the various trophies in the room.

I had to hand it to her. She knew better than anyone how to flutter her eyelids and persuade men to talk to her. I acknowledged her skill with a smile of thanks.

"Fiona told me that Mr. McLean was bringing a new trophy head today." I glanced up at the bare spot on the wall above our heads. "But I guess that didn't happen after all, on account of all that was going on today."

"Naw," Rosenquist said with a chuckle as he turned back around, "he didn't come because he knows *I'm* here."

"Why should that matter?" I said. "He referred you to Woody, that's what you said. And also to Officer Lester."

"Let's just say our dealings have been less than simpatico."

Rosenquist and Lester folded their arms across their chests and exchanged glances. What was going on here? Was the taxidermy shop on the take? That could explain why a police officer maybe had become involved with McLean at some point in the past.

I wouldn't let it alone. "Are you suggesting that McLean knows something about the poachers?"

"What would be the point of adding anymore trophies," the game warden said with a nod at the wall, "now that Woody's gone?"

It was a classic diversion tactic if I ever heard one. He was trying to change the subject. "But if McLean knows who the poacher is," I said, "why doesn't he just tell you?"

"Claims he doesn't know," Lester said.

Rosenquist grunted. "It's not in his interest to know."

"Why not?" I said. "Doesn't he care if his subjects were poached?"

Stony silence answered me, and then Jill jumped in. "Nell just means that we don't understand such complicated matters, not the way you do."

Lester scratched his head. "Well, it *is* complicated. You see, it's a craft to him. He doesn't want to know where his supply comes from. His taxidermy business would suffer too much."

Wow. "That's an excuse?" I said. "He doesn't want to turn in his suppliers and cut off his income stream?"

"Of course not," Rosenquist said, slapping the table. "If we arrest one of his sources, someone else will step in and take his place. We're going to do this right and put them all out of business."

"How would you do that?" Jill asked sweetly.

"There's a dealer," Lester said, "who brings the product to him, and then usually finds the buyer. And takes a cut. McLean only deals with a go-between."

Apparently, it was all about money. If McLean turned in the dealer, then everyone would lose money. I could understand the fear of losing one's income, but honestly, poverty was better than the evil that drove poachers. It had to be more than a lust for money. Was it self above all?

I still didn't get it. "Then why did he refer you to a detective? Wouldn't that ruin his set-up?"

"I'll get him to talk," Rosenquist said. "Off the record, of course. And when I gather the evidence against him, I'll bring in the ringleader who's driving the market. His operatives will fall apart without him."

So that's why Rosenquist had appeared so "helpful" earlier, volunteering to escort Dr. Newman back into the horse stalls. He wanted to snoop around, maybe see what interesting evidence he could find among Blaze's things. But he was sniffing in the wrong place. Crossbows were legal now, Jerry Lester the game warden had said.

Besides, the Pollyanna in me wanted to believe that Blaze was too young and naïve to get involved with a racket like poaching.

It was one more case that Rosenquist would bungle.

Then, inspiration struck. Maybe that's why the taxidermist wanted this particular detective to do the so-called investigating. Because he knew Rosenquist would blow it.

And then McLean could breathe easy.

Not Woody, though. Had Woody died because he knew who the poacher was?

* * *

At the dinner table, we were still waiting for the rest of our salads to arrive when a movement in the doorway caught my attention. It was Libby, motioning me to her, where she stood beside the glass doors into the reception lounge. I excused myself and crossed the room, feeling Jill's curious gaze upon my back. She was too busy with her male admirers to volunteer to accompany me.

Libby shrank back into the lobby, and I followed. In the muted light of the fireplace and antler lamps, her face looked pale.

"You've got to come see this for yourself," she whispered. Turning, she darted across the lounge toward the hallway that led to our guestrooms.

I had to hurry to keep up with her pace. She sped along the carpet runner to Willow's door, where the do-not-disturb sign still hung from its handle. The door stood open.

From the hall, there was nothing to see inside besides the usual hotel room furniture. The bedcovers looked rumpled, as if someone had lain there recently.

"This is how I found her room," Libby said, stepping aside for me to enter.

I gave her a cautious glance. Something had apparently disturbed Willow. Leaning across the threshold, I called out. "Willow?"

There was no response.

No soft sounds of anyone breathing.

No whiffs of body oils to indicate someone's presence.

Still, I remained alert to my peripheral vision as I slowly entered the guestroom. The bathroom door also stood open, showing us nothing more than the fixtures, a bar of soap, and used towels draped across the tub's rim. "Where is she?"

"I don't know," Libby said from behind me. "When I came to check on her, the door was ajar and the room was like this. I didn't see her. I wonder if her things are still here?"

"Let's find out." I strode over to the closet and slid the folding door to one side.

No backpack. Nothing hung from the hangers. I whirled around, crossed over to the dresser, and pulled open its drawers. They were empty, too.

"Do you think she just left?" Libby asked. "Didn't she say anything to you?"

"Not a word."

"That doesn't sound good," Libby said. "She should've told you she was leaving, even if she didn't tell anyone else."

I agreed. "She must've been in quite a hurry."

"Not so much," Libby said, "if she had enough time to pack up her things."

I frowned. "Then, maybe she couldn't tell us."

"Why not?" Libby said. "She could've at least left a note. I don't see one, do you? Maybe... You don't think... Did she run away because she thought that sheriff really *did* want to arrest her?"

I shook my head no, mostly to ease Libby's worries. But I had to concede that none of us really knew anyone else in the group very well. For all I knew, there could be something else in Willow's background that she didn't want to come out as a result of an investigation.

"Let's go see if her car is still here," I said, turning away. We'd all ridden up together in Willow's SUV today.

We hurried down the hall and pushed through the front

door, onto the porch. Night had fallen. Animals would be lurking not far away in the forest that surrounded us. I dug in my pocket for my key chain, which held a small flashlight, and flicked it on. We followed the pencil thin trail of light as it bobbed down the steps and across crunching gravel toward the parking lot. Past the row of pine trees, I swept the light across the vehicles parked there. There were only two. And Willow's SUV was not one of them.

Chapter Eleven

The night air felt thick around us.

Libby sucked in her breath. "Oh no! She's bailed on us!"

It certainly looked that way. I had no words of comfort to offer Libby. Willow had taken off. Had something frightened her into running away?

We stood in silence for several heartbeats, taking it in. Night insects, birds, and reptiles whistled and clicked around us.

Libby finally said, "Maybe she had to get to a lower altitude quick on account of her headache. Altitude sickness is nothing to fool with. Do you think it was getting worse, and that's why she left?"

"Maybe." But I didn't believe it, and I didn't think Libby did, either. I kept telling myself that Willow would be back. But then there was her room, empty of all her things. Alongside Libby, I kept staring at the nearly empty parking lot.

"Maybe she ran away," Libby said, her voice choking, "because of something that frightened her about Woody's accident. Or something she wants to hide."

I agreed that looked possible.

She went on. "But what's there to hide? It was an accident. The sheriff said so. He said Woody got too close to that moose."

"That doesn't make him right."

"You don't believe the sheriff!" she said with a gasp. "You think there's more to it than that, don't you?"

I did.

I was as sure it was murder as Libby wanted desperately to believe it was an accident. It was wishful thinking on her part, but as for me, I was becoming conditioned to murder. I was the Typhoid Mary of murder. For the last six months, the crime rate of our relatively peaceful and naïve hometown had been rising everywhere I went.

Good thing I'd left town.

But now murder had followed me here. What else could Woody's death be but murder?

"Maybe Andrea was right," Libby said. "Maybe they've arrested Willow."

"Her car would still be here if Gustafson had taken her into custody." I tried to reason with this student of mine. "She wouldn't have driven herself to jail."

Libby edged closer to me. "I hope that Andrea and the rest of them are wrong, but what else can you expect them to think? Willow leaving in such a hurry makes her look guilty of something, even if she's not. She was the last one to see Woody alive. And it was no secret what she thought about Woody. You can't imagine the terrible things she said about him while we were getting to know each other today."

"She wasn't the only one who didn't like him." I hadn't liked the man, either. He had been easy to dislike. "But that isn't enough grounds for murder."

"You shouldn't say that word," Libby said, her voice catching on a sob when I uttered the m-word. "Even if Willow was somehow responsible for it, it was still an accident. Let's just accept that the sheriff was right, okay?"

I shrugged, not accepting anything point blank, and put my arm around her. She was trembling. "Gustafson was in a hurry to get home. Even if he wants to arrest her, he's not going to do anything about it until tomorrow, at the earliest."

"Which is exactly why she would've run off tonight," Libby said, "before he can do anything."

"We'll see what the situation looks like in the morning," I said. "Maybe Willow will have returned by then. Let's go back to dinner now. There's not much else we can do in the meanwhile."

Libby sniffed. "Oh yes we can. We'd better figure out how we're going to get home without Willow to drive us."

I tugged her arm, pulling her back towards the ranch house. "There's another car coming up in the morning."

"But it won't have enough room to hold all of us," Libby said. "We were already cramped enough in Willow's big car, plus all that gear we brought along."

The tools of my trade, that's what she meant. If she was suggesting I ditch my bags of protective padding and stacks of mats, she was wrong. Better to think that we were stranded here in the mountains with a killer on the loose. Oh joy.

"Can we rent a car somewhere?" Libby said. "Maybe in that cute little town we passed when we turned off the main road?"

I snorted. "Not likely."

Libby pulled away from me, stopping in the middle of the driveway. "I have to be back at work Monday morning."

So did I, assuming I still had a job by then.

"How could she do this to us?" Libby went on with a wail.

"She probably had a good reason."

"I doubt it," Libby said with a sniff. "Now we'll have to call someone who can come get us. Maybe a Lyft. Do they come this far into the mountains?"

I had no idea.

"You must know someone," she said. "I don't know anyone. I only moved to Boulder last month."

I sighed. She was right about one thing. It was my responsibility to get my group back home. But who could I call? My daughter Terra only had a learner's permit, and my best friend Alice didn't have a car. My boss, Mr. Callahan, was almost always inaccessible. His secretary, Poppy, kept pointing out how much Mr. Callahan appreciated initiative in his employees. I suspected it was because he didn't want to deal with us.

Poppy...

I wondered what kind of car she drove?

But weekends were her well-deserved time off. I couldn't ruin that for her.

That left Dad.

Except, I couldn't endanger him. Ask him—or any of them, for that matter—to come up here before the murderer was caught? No way.

But I knew it was only a question of time before Dad would find out. He always did. Dad had special radar.

* * *

Goosebumps crawled over me as we went back inside the ranch house. And not just on account of our discoveries so far. It was downright chilly at nine thousand plus feet in elevation after the sun went down. Woody's death made it feel even chillier.

Libby and I made a pact not to alarm the others just yet with the distressing news of Willow's disappearance. My stomach churned through the rest of dinner, and I ended up only nibbling at my venison stew. It was probably delectable, given the savory smells of onions and who knew what else Fiona had thrown in, but my mind kept twisting through our various problems.

Libby retreated behind her shy demeanor again. She'd singled me out, having waved me away from the dinner table, to handle the problem. Problems were my specialty. That's what I was here for.

And soon, Dad...

I'd better start steeling myself now for the backlash of Dad riding to my rescue. He was sure I shouldn't be out in the big, wicked world on my own, and if he had to rescue me, I wouldn't hear the end of it. But I wouldn't let him even try, not until the murderer was taken care of. If I ever wanted to get home, I needed to figure out who really was our culprit.

"Pssst," Jill said, catching my attention, only to shake her head at me. "No."

I scowled back. I couldn't not think about it.

Okay, so who was our culprit?

Whether or not the events surrounding Woody's death really were accidental, Gustafson had tried his best to convince us that it had been an accident between Woody and a moose. Why would he try so hard to do that if he really suspected murder? Was I wrong? Or...

Maybe he hadn't wanted us to become overly alarmed about having a murderer in our midst.

And if Willow had stumbled across the murderer, then maybe she'd run away fearing for her life. As Kitty apparently had.

And that left the rest of us exactly where?

Somehow, dinner finished while I stewed and Jill eyed me. Game Warden Lester thanked us for our company, peeled himself away from Jill, and excused himself. I wondered how many mountain passes he had to cross before he made it back to his home, wherever that was. Rosenquist walked him out. My ears pricked up to the crunching sounds of gravel, but they were retreating sounds. It was Lester's vehicle leaving. No one arriving. Willow was still gone.

Judging from the looks on my students' faces, their stomachs were full. Mine rumbled. Jill always ate like a bird. We all cleared our plates and pitched in to wash up. Rosenquist still didn't return.

And what had he been doing here in the first place? Back in the barn, he'd seemed in a hurry to leave. Had Gustafson asked him to remain with us in order to observe us?

In other words, he was a spy.

Or maybe he was supposed to be our bodyguard, protecting us in case the killer decided to strike again. I kept that thought to myself. No use inviting panic.

When we finally had everything spic and span, Libby emerged from her shyness to propose a bit of stargazing before we called it a night.

"You go on ahead," I said. "I have to make a phone call first. Got to check in with the kid, y'know." Since my antique cell phone didn't get reception here, I would have to use Woody's landline.

I tried not to think about a possible murderer on the loose. My gang had safety in numbers on their side, and I wouldn't be away from the stargazers very long. Jill lingered with me, but I sent her along with the others.

Some minutes later, their bubbling laughter faded as my gang disappeared through the glass doors into the lobby and out the front door. I lagged behind, lingering alone in the dining room. Not entirely alone. It was me and a dozen or so heads staring at me from the wall.

"What do you think?" I asked the boys.

They didn't tell me. Truth be told, I was procrastinating, not overly eager for Dad to hijack the phone from Terra. He would remind me of all the potential pitfalls surrounding me. Putting off this encounter, I let my mind spin over all that I knew. Or rather, *didn't* know. The points didn't add up.

First point: Woody had had his rifle with him. He would've shot a moose before letting it get close enough to trample him. But he hadn't. Why not?

Out of deference to the laws of hunting season? No offense to the dead, but I had a hard time picturing Woody deferent to anything. What else could explain his failure to shoot the moose?

Maybe, I answered myself, it happened too fast.

But according to Fiona, he was up there specifically looking for the moose, my counterpoint went. Woody would've been ready for that moose. If Gustafson was right that the moose had trampled Woody, causing his death, I doubted it was by accident. But no murderer could've guided a moose into doing what it had done.

Which led me to my next point: Something clearly surprised Woody.

Something he hadn't been expecting had surprised him so badly that he hadn't been able to shoot the moose before getting trampled. Why not? Had he been knocked out first, therefore unable to shoot?

The boys on the wall didn't help me solve anything, so I gave them a nod goodnight and straggled toward the glass door. I wasn't sure what I was going to tell Dad, once his radar honed in on my problems. I'd better think of something fast.

Someone was already there, standing in front of the registration desk, his back turned to me as he shuffled papers on the counter. I recognized his squat build, his khaki trousers, his flannel shirt and camouflage vest. It was Rosenquist.

Chapter Twelve

The fireplace crackled as I stood there in the doorway to the reception lounge. "Oh!" I said, by way of announcing my presence. Rosenquist's hunched body language told me he was engaged in furtive activity. "I thought you'd left."

Which made my spy hypothesis more likely than the bodyguard theory.

His shoulders flinched, and the piece of paper he'd been holding dropped onto the counter of the desk he was bending over. He snapped a file folder shut. Several others lay strewn before him. He swiveled around to face me. His eyes glittered as he squinted at me in the glow from the hearth.

"Yeah? What is it, Mrs. Gannon?"

"You looking for something, Detective?" He wasn't a detective any more than I was a Gannon.

"Is that any business of yours?"

"Maybe I can help," I said, thinking fast. I'd seen someone else bending over that very spot—Kitty. She'd been looking for something here, too, earlier today. The same thing that Rosenquist wanted now?

He grunted, and one corner of his mouth twisted in what might've been a grin. "Why the offer? You think you know something about Woody's filing system? I bet you made that your business, too."

"Are you suggesting I'm a snoop?" That was the kindest thing he'd ever said to me. I chose to feel flattered, rather than insulted. Usually, he didn't think I was capable of anything.

"You'll think what you want. With this mess, it's no wonder the man's business was failing." Rosenquist swept his arm, indicating the assortment of file folders covering the ledger book on the registration counter.

Was the ranch business failing, I wondered? Was that why we'd managed to obtain accommodations at this prime time of the season? But regardless of the state of the ranch's financial health, what did it matter to Rosenquist? Or to Kitty, for that matter?

"Those file folders," I said, "weren't here when I came through the lobby before dinner."

"Of course they weren't, Mrs. Gannon. I pulled them out just now."

"You need some help going through them?" Here I was, being Sherlock, and offering to *help* this annoying man.

"Never mind." He scooped the folders into a sloppy pile and tucked them under his arm.

"Kitty was looking for something, too," I said, blurting it out before thinking.

"Oh? Kitty *Robin*?" His arms twitched, and one of the folders slipped from his grip, falling to the floor. He swore, clutching the rest tightly, frowning, as if on the edge of disaster.

"That's the one." I dropped to my knees to gather up the newspaper clippings that had scattered around the spilled folder.

"I'll do that," he said, snapping at me. He tossed the rest

of the bundle back onto the counter and joined me on the floor, grabbing the clippings from my hand.

"I was just helping." I wasn't really surprised by his brusque chastisement, but I felt wounded all the same. "Why are these clippings so important?" I turned my head to the right and the left, scanning them as he snatched them away. They showed photos of bears and elk and mountain lions.

"They aren't."

Some of the photos included figures holding rifles. "You seem to think they're important. And so did Kitty."

And furthermore, I thought, biting my tongue to prevent me from saying it out loud, it was the mention of Kitty and her interest just now that had upset him enough to drop his grip on the sought-after but unimportant clippings. So clearly, the contents of the file folders were important. Why did he think I wouldn't figure it out?

He grumbled. "She doesn't know anything." He stuffed the clippings back into the folder and rose.

"It seems to me," I said, standing also and facing him, chin to chin, "that she must know something, and that's why she's left and hasn't returned."

"She'll be back, trust me on that."

"Sounds like you know her pretty well." Then I realized, and my cheeks flamed with my realization: There'd been a reason why Rosenquist had chosen this particular area of the mountains in which to fish, following his departure from Boulder's police department. Kitty was that reason. He'd been chasing after a woman. How un-Rosenquist-like.

"I've dealt with her enough times," he said.

Romantically? My face must've betrayed the wonder of

my thoughts, given his snort.

"Not like that," he said.

"A-ha." The man had no family. Probably no friends, either. Therefore, I deduced that his encounters with Kitty would've been the result of his official capacity. What else could it be? Cops pursued crooks. Did that mean she was a crook? And if so, then had she been in the process of stealing something from Woody? Maybe Rosenquist was only trying to protect whatever that thing was from her pilfering.

"I doubt if she wanted these clippings," I said. "She was looking in the ledger book. It's hard to believe he actually kept one. Woody, I mean. How old-fashioned is that?"

"Enough to ruin his business. He couldn't keep up with the times."

"You think Kitty was after him for that?" I was trying to follow the flow of his logic.

"I don't think anything, and neither do you." He grabbed the file folders off the counter and marched across the lobby, toward the front door. "They'll want to talk to you in the morning, Mrs. Gannon, so make sure you're still here. Good night." He slammed the door shut behind him.

I stared at the square of glass in the door's panel for several beats. Even if I wanted to leave, where would I go at this hour without transportation? I could go bear hunting, and that was about it.

My hasty accusations echoed back at me through my mind. Kitty? Had I really accused her of being involved in something crooked? I rued my flippant tongue. But at the same time...

It was true that she had left the ranch, presumably looking

for Fiona, but she had lied about what she knew—according to Fiona. And it was also true that Kitty had fled after her argument with Blaze. Now Rosenquist seemed to be covering something up, wanting me not to suspect Kitty.

I had riled him up by interrupting his search. In my experience, he'd never recouped well from surprises.

He must've figured it out, that it had been no accident that had killed Woody. He must agree with my suspicions of murder.

Except, he was supposed to be tracking the poacher.

Feeling somewhat vindicated—it wasn't just me, being paranoid—I reached for the phone on the counter of the registration desk and dialed my Dad's farmhouse down on the plains east of Boulder. It took him several rings to pick up, and I could picture Dad grumbling, struggling out of his recliner, pulled away from his favorite program on TV. It was Thursday night, so... *Uh-oh.*

His voice barked at me, as growly as Rosenquist's had been. "We don't want any," he said.

"Dad, it's me," I said quickly. "Don't hang up."

"Nellie? What's wrong?"

I could almost hear the wheels spinning in his head. Normally, I knew better than to call him in the middle of his favorite television program. That I had lapsed surely indicated something out of the normal.

"Nothing's wrong, Dad." The heat of a flush rose to my face from my lie. "I just need to talk to Terra. Is she there?" Of course my teenaged daughter was there. She'd better be there. It was a school night.

Dad grumbled some more, and I heard the muffled

sounds of his calling to my daughter, which made me wonder why she hadn't picked up in the first place. Whenever the phone rang, Terra was usually on it.

Her voice came over the line. "Hi Mom, how's it going?"

We exchanged a few pleasantries—she told me about the total unfairness of her history teacher's expectations, while I told her we'd seen a moose. I skipped the part about it nearly running us down, and about the arrow, too. Somehow, I failed to mention anything about the fate of Woody.

"So, honey," I said, moving on to the point where I had to butter her up. "You know how you're like a wizard when it comes to finding things on the internet?"

Silence answered me. I was beginning to think the connection had dropped when she finally spoke. "What's up, Mom? What do you want me to find for you?"

"Do you remember that detective who questioned me about the murder of the guy who was the instructor at Callahan's before me?"

"You mean, that cop who thought you killed my dad?"

"That's the one." I paused for a beat, as the memory of Rosenquist's unfairness and his unrelenting suspicions washed through me. "I gather it wasn't the first time he'd acted, shall we say, unprofessionally?"

"Right, and he got sacked for it. What about him?"

"Well, guess where he's turned up?"

"No way! He's there with you?" Terra shrieked, then mumbled an apology to her grandfather.

Scratching sounds came over the line, and then Dad's voice yelled at me. "Nellie? What's going on? I knew something was wrong."

124

"Dad, everything is okay. I can handle it. Please put Terra back on the line. You don't want to miss your show."

He grumbled some more, and then Terra spoke again. "What do you want me to find out about him?"

"If he had anything to do with a case about a woman by the name of Kitty Robin. Something that might have to do with wild animals? And I believe Kitty might have a twin sister by the name of Kirby. Look for any connections at all, honey. I want to know what brought him to this particular corner of the mountains. I think something about Kitty—or her sister—brought him up here."

"And this has exactly what to do with your moose?"

My daughter always saw right through me. I covered up with a chuckle. "Nothing, likely. But I guess it might be possible. Can you do it?"

"Cake. When do you need it? I've got a test tomorrow that I'm booking for now."

"The sooner the better, but your studies come first..." I hesitated. I could almost hear the clock ticking to get this murderer behind bars.

"What aren't you telling me, Mom?"

"Nothing, honey. Good luck on your test. And don't forget to get a full night's sleep." Feeling guilty that I'd dumped the task onto her, I let her get back to her studying. I hung up the phone, stared at it for a couple minutes, and then headed for the front door, in search of my stargazing students.

Was I asking too much of my daughter? She'd helped me before, and had seemed pleased—mostly—that her technical knowledge outshone her mom's. She was a good student at school, just shy of stellar, so I always wanted to encourage those things that she was good at—like the technical stuff. If Terra's skill could help me find the connection between Kitty, Rosenquist, and the poachers who seemed to be at the heart of the mystery of Woody's death, then I felt sure that I would be on my way to its solution. As long as Terra stayed long distance, she would stay out of harm's way.

Did that leave me in the path of danger?

Was that danger the reason why Willow had left?

I pushed my way through the front door, across the porch, and down onto the gravel of the driveway. The pine trees stood like forlorn sentinels over the empty parking lot. The last of the vehicles—Rosenquist's—was gone. So much for my idea that he was supposed to spy on us.

Across from that empty parking area, I found my group on the knoll where the driveway fell away to the valley below. Libby was pointing overhead, speaking with hushed wonder in her voice. I looked up.

The Milky Way streamed overhead, looking like a river of glowing clouds. Without the interference of city lights, the star-studded sky up here in the mountains dazzled me. No wonder the ancients made up stories about the patterns of lights.

I sank onto a rock to listen to Libby's retelling of the ancients' stories. A contented, somnolent state washed over me. Thank goodness we were nearing the end of a long and difficult day.

Although relaxed, I was only listening with half an ear to Libby and her stories about the night sky. Suspicions haunted me throughout the *oohs* and *ahhs* that Harlan, Andrea, and Jill mumbled. Every once in a while, I echoed their awe, just to let them know I was present.

Then Libby pointed out the constellation of Pegasus, and I jolted back to attention. The legend she told us about the flying horse described how it reared up after a sting from a gadfly, throwing its rider.

Could that possibly explain what had happened today?

It was possible that a stinging insect—or some other fright—had caused Kitty's horse to rear up and strike Woody. If that was the case, not even Kitty, an experienced rider, would have been able to control her horse.

Kitty and her horse had been up there at the lake. Both Fiona and Rosenquist had said so. And Butterscotch had sustained injuries that the vet was treating.

It all made sense.

Something had surprised Woody, and that surprise had ended in his death. He hadn't fought the surprise because maybe it was something he cared about. Like Kitty's horse, Butterscotch.

What if Woody's death had been a terrible accident after all? Not deliberate. Not murder.

Chapter Thirteen

Later, in my room, I couldn't sleep. Willow still hadn't returned, and I felt terrible, thinking that I'd suspected murder. Voices haunted me as I shifted in my bed, trying to read myself to sleep, but it was all to no avail.

You shouldn't say that word, Libby had said, trying to warn me not to think murder.

I could almost hear the gently chiding voice of my sensei, Master Hwang...

Look for the hidden truths in what you see, as it may not be what you expect.

As if I expected murder. Well, I had, hadn't I?

And I heard another voice in my head, less gentle and more on the nagging side. Jill always told me that I fixated on murder too much.

It's not healthy, she usually complained.

I had never been healthier in my life.

But it was true that finding six dead bodies in six months would tend to make a person assume the worst.

All along, I had been wrong. This time, death was caused by an accident, I was almost sure of it now. And felt terrible for the awful thoughts I'd poured into poor Libby's head. Shame on me for doubting deputy sheriff Gustafson's word.

Then I heard something else, not an imaginary voice but something real this time. Floorboards creaked. Either the building was settling, or there were furtive footsteps in the hall. My book tumbled shut as I lifted up from the downy nest of my pillows. I listened for a while, but nothing else sounded. No doors clicked shut. No voices in the hall. Leaning back, I found my place again in my book.

But the voices inside my head kept badgering me.

Why hadn't Kitty simply said it was an accident? Why had she run away instead of seeking help for Woody? And why had she deceived us, pretending not to know what happened to him?

Now a new sound broke into my mental dispute. This time, it *was* something else, an unearthly call coming from outdoors, and I couldn't quite identify it. The sound drifted through my tightly closed windowpane. A bugling elk? I didn't think they bugled this late at night. Coyotes, maybe. I came to attention, listening. No, it almost sounded... musical. Like the very faint twang of... a guitar?

I listened harder, but the sound didn't repeat. I'd seen a guitar in one of the photos of Edna, Woody's dead wife, over in the barn, in his horse-stall office. Had I imagined hearing one now?

Most likely, it was a coyote.

My thoughts returned to Kitty as my unread book balanced across my chest. Perhaps guilt had paralyzed her, leaving her unable to confess about her role in Woody's accident.

Or... Maybe she had something to hide.

The coyote howled again.

I tossed aside my book, clicked off my reading light, and

threw back my covers. I climbed out of bed and stumbled across my darkened room to the window, as if I could spot the coyote jamboree. Of course I couldn't. My window overlooked the barn, where I'd seen the quarrel between Kitty and Blaze. All looked quiet now. The ranch had bedded down for the night, and yet...

A light flickered through a narrow window in the barn. A small, faint, ghostly light... More than likely, it was just a reflection, bouncing off a source that I couldn't see through the window. From something small, like a flashlight. It dimmed as I watched, as if the person using it had covered the light with his hand. It looked suspiciously like someone who did not wish to be seen.

Willow? Or maybe it was Edna's ghost.

Chills swept over me. I didn't believe in ghosts. Something real had drawn me here to the window. A coyote. And something else.

Bottom line: *someone else was still up this late, and that someone had something to hide.*

Dousing my curiosity was like sprinkling oil on a kitchen fire.

I justified my investigation as an opportunity to correct my wrongs. Besides, if there had been no murder, then there was no murderer, either. No worries, right?

I tugged my sweats on over my tee-shirt nightie, dropped my old-fashioned room key into the handwarmer pocket, and stepped into flip-flops. I slipped out of my room and darted down the hall. Passing Willow's room, I noticed that her door was closed and the do-not-disturb sign had disappeared.

She'd hung it there this afternoon, claiming to nurse a

headache—or someone else had hung it—but she really went up to the lake with Woody. She—or someone—didn't want the rest of us to know that she was with Woody. Why not? Had she needed an alibi because she had intended harm to Woody?

I shook myself, reminding myself that I meant to prove Willow's innocence, not support the idea of her guilt.

The footsteps I'd heard a short while ago had hopefully been Willow, sneaking back, after whatever she'd been up to that had taken her away from dinner.

Continuing on down the hall, I held my breath as I rushed past Jill's room. I didn't want to disturb her and raise more alarms. As I passed her door, something wooden squeaked, and I nearly jumped out of my flip-flops.

"Pssst," someone hissed. Jill's door cracked open, and dim light leaked out around a shadowy sliver of my almost-sis.

Busted.

"Are you up?" Jill said, her words barely a whisper. She opened the door wider. "Want a nightcap?"

I followed her inside, and she shut and bolted the door behind us. She headed to the dresser, where one antler lamp glowed softly, and poured her favorite drink—a twenty-year tawny port—into two plastic hotel cups. Tufts of her usually perfectly-coifed blonde hair slipped loose from crooked clips, and... good grief, her silk robe of red paisleys didn't match her pink, fluffball slippers. What was wrong with her? I had never seen Jill in anything less than perfect coordination, including her nails, even at bedtime. She handed me my drink with a trembling hand.

"Jill, honey!" I said. "What's up?"

"I don't know, Nell. You tell me."

I sniffed my port. "Are you drinking enough water?"

"Lord, yes. Washing up after all my trips to the toilet is going to ruin my nails."

"Then, what is it?"

Jill shuddered and glanced over her shoulder at the drapes, drawn tightly closed across her window. "It's this place. Didn't you hear them? The coyotes? It's like they're circling around us, and at any moment they're going to charge us and eat us all up."

"No they won't. They don't do that. Anyway, you're perfectly safe inside."

She burst out laughing and saluted me with her drink. She'd been teasing me, and I let out a sigh of relief. I laughed with her and then sipped my drink. It slid down my throat a little too fast.

"Seriously though," she said, "*you* weren't going to stay inside. I just knew you'd go out prowling. You can never resist. And besides, I heard footsteps."

"They weren't mine."

"Of course they were. You can't deny it. I caught you."

"I only just now left my room. Not before."

She ran her fingers through her hair and refastened a clip. "What are you saying? It wasn't you I heard?"

"Nope, not me."

"Well, that just goes to prove it, doesn't it? About this place, I mean. I knew it. How do you do it, Nell? How do you always manage to insert yourself into the middle of these things?"

I shrugged, not sure myself.

"Well, now that you're in deep," she said, "we've got to

get you out, don't we? And the sooner the better, because I'm seeing my boyfriend Sean on Sunday night."

Jill had a different set of priorities than mine, but I could always count on her to watch my back. Good old Jill. "No kidding," I said.

She refilled my glass. "All right, what have we got?"

"Woody's dead, and the sheriff thinks it was an accident. I don't believe it."

"Don't remind me. I'm not sure I believe him, either, not with that crazy story about a moose trampling him. Can they even do that?"

I assured her that a massive animal like a moose definitely could. "But I think whoever killed him wanted to make it look that way. Why?"

Jill shrugged. "And how could anyone want to kill a nice old man like Woody?"

"Yeah, that's what you might think, but he condoned poaching. That didn't make him so nice."

"You think that's why someone killed him?"

"Maybe to cover up something," I said. "Or maybe to keep Woody from uncovering something—like the poacher's identity. Or a secret." There seemed to be a lot of secrets here at Woody's ranch.

"The poacher did it." Jill sounded certain.

I had to admit that I was leaning toward that theory. The poacher was a likely possibility. "We don't know who the poacher is. Maybe he's someone right under our nose. Someone here at the ranch. Maybe he's a she. If he can kill animals, he can probably kill people, too."

"That makes him capable," Jill said.

"But why would he risk his poaching business by committing murder?"

"Good point. Who else, then?"

"Maybe," I said, "it was someone protecting the poacher."

"Like who?"

I sipped my port slowly, while other possibilities tumbled through my mind. "Well, there's Fiona."

Jill scoffed. "I don't think much of her as a killer. She's too frumpy."

"I didn't think fashion was a prerequisite for murder."

"Okay, then, you can call her 'too nice.' She's like anyone's mother. Look what she was doing for Woody, helping out to make his trophy display just perfect for him. And she's strong, too." Jill ticked off her points on the manicured tips of her fingers.

"She's not all that nice," I said. "She didn't like Woody very much. And she really has a low opinion of men in general. Must've been burned pretty badly." Max, my ex, came to mind, but I blinked him away from my thoughts and rubbed a tear from my face.

Jill narrowed her jade eyes to slits. "The sheriff seems to think your student, Willow, is the prime suspect. What do you really know about her?"

"Nothing. But it doesn't look so good for her. She left a do-not-disturb sign on her door today while she was out with Woody, as if she was trying to create an alibi for herself, making people think she was here. Or maybe someone else did, someone who was collaborating with her."

"That was me."

"You?" I breathed another sigh of relief. My suspicions

blew up in my face.

Jill shrugged. "She and I stayed behind while you were out on your hike, remember? She said she was going to nap, but she forgot to hang that little sign on her door. So I did it for her. How was I to know she wasn't really in her room at all? You'd better watch that girl. Don't be too sure about her."

"If she wants to learn martial arts, that makes her okay in my book."

"Don't be so obtuse, Nell. I swear, sometimes it's like you wear blinders. Didn't you notice her little tirade? She thinks that anyone who collects antlers—like Woody did—was creating the market to encourage poachers. She wanted to stop that."

"She wants to relocate prairie dogs, too."

"Sure, but so do a lot of people," Jill said, spilling a drop of her port in her agitation. "There's also the fact that she was the last person to see Woody alive. Don't forget that. You can't argue with facts. That last person is always the one who does it."

"Technically, yes. But obviously, the real killer saw Woody alive after Willow left him. Besides, she didn't even know him until today when we arrived here."

"You don't really know that for a fact. You don't know anything about her."

"True," I said, "but let's look at other possibilities. There's Blaze. He's the most logical suspect, because he stands to inherit the ranch."

Jill flounced to the dresser and splashed more port into her cup. "He's too cute to be a killer. And anyway, he's too young. All he has to do is wait a few more years, and he'll inherit naturally, without having to go to jail in the meanwhile for murder. Woody couldn't have lasted too many more years, not with the way he smoked. And did you happen to notice his gut?"

"Maybe Woody was going to change his will and Blaze had to stop that from happening."

"You're fishing, Nell. Just to be contrary. I'll tell you who's most likely. That Kitty person. Did you happen to notice her boots? They're last year's fashion. And those jeans? Where on earth did she buy them? They don't fit, either, and—"

"Hang on. Since when does one's fashion determine guilt?"

"Just sayin'. You should open your eyes sometime, girl. Give me one good reason why she's not your guy."

I was sure there was a good reason, but at the moment, I couldn't recall it. All I could think of was the way Kitty had deceived us. She'd already known about Woody's death before she joined the rest of us in the reception lounge. Yet, she had acted surprised, as if she didn't know about it at all. I thought hard, but I couldn't come up with a good explanation for that little deceit. All I knew for sure was that whatever had happened up there, she clearly had something to hide.

Chapter Fourteen

Handing over my half-full cup to Jill, I said goodnight and slipped out of her room. The extra port gave her something else to think about, so she didn't protest. She probably thought I was going back to bed.

I wasn't.

Kitty harbored secrets. Had she been the one I'd seen through my bedroom window a short while ago? Someone had been in the barn with a flashlight before my detour with Jill. If I hurried, maybe I could find out.

In the reception lounge, the front door to the ranch was locked with a single bolt that released easily with a twist. I crept outside, holding my breath with each click and squeak, and paused on the porch, listening for coyotes. Heard none.

Wait. I did hear something, but not an animal's howl. It was very faint. Voices? A soft laugh?

Someone else hadn't been able to sleep.

As my eyes adjusted to the dark, the stars lit up the driveway. The row of pine trees, their branches waving in the breeze, stood like guards over the parking lot. I couldn't help but notice that a car had shown up. It gleamed silver, looking a lot like Willow's SUV.

She really was back. I let out my breath in a sigh of relief.

And breathed in a whiff of... smoke?

Not good.

Smoke meant fire, and fire was definitely not compatible with our dry mountains. We usually had a fire ban in place, and I tried to remember if I'd seen the signs indicating a ban on our way up here. I'd grown so accustomed to seeing those signs that I didn't even notice them anymore. Not good.

If something had caught fire, I would have to sound the alarm. Maybe that's what the coyotes had been yelling about. Thank goodness for my sleeplessness. Tugging my sweatshirt tighter around me, I stepped down off the porch and onto the graveled driveway, rocks poking through my rubber soles. I headed toward the knoll where we had stargazed a few hours ago. It offered an unobstructed view of the valley in the distance and the mountain peaks surrounding us in the shape of a horseshoe.

Along the way, I heard the voices again, sounding as if they were coming from one of the sheds that dotted the property. Someone else was out here, and surely they'd also smelled the smoke. Perhaps they'd already alerted our brave firefighters. It was a good thing Willow had returned—now we had a vehicle at our disposal in case we had to evacuate. And I wouldn't have to confess my car-less situation to Dad.

I followed the soft sound of voices to one of the sheds. I hated to interrupt their rendezvous, but fire was a serious matter, and I needed to know what these people knew about it.

Light flickered from the far side of the shed, and I hurried my step. Rounding the corner, I stopped in mid-step. It was a fire pit, the flames contained in a round, clay oven. No open fire, after all. My heart rate settled, and I breathed again.

Two figures hunched over the pit, watching the dancing

flames. They held bottles, probably of beer, given the rising lilt to their voices.

I faded back into the shadows that hugged the side of the shed, not wishing to interrupt them now that I saw that the source of the smoke was a controlled fire.

"Where's Mitchell?" one of them said.

Mitchell? Who the heck was Mitchell? I didn't know, but my curiosity pricked even more on account of the soft, lilting voice. It was a woman, and she sounded a lot like Kitty.

Kitty had been gone all afternoon and evening. Where had she been? Her absence only added fuel to the suspicions I'd just cooked up with Jill. I started to step away from the protection of the shed and demand some information, but something clandestine about their manner held me back.

The other person grunted and took a swig from his bottle. "Mitchell ain't here." Blaze.

"I can see that, you dope," Kitty said. "He was supposed to bring it in. The truck is waiting around back."

"Maybe he couldn't find it."

Flames from the fire pit glowed, illuminating the two of them. Kitty sprang to her feet, her long ponytail whipping around her. I plastered myself against the splintery wood of the shed.

"Because of *her*," Kitty said. "You should've stopped her."

"How was I to know? She didn't ask me. She just took off and went out on her own."

"And screwed everything up, thank you very much."

"She don't know how to shoot," Blaze said.

"She wasn't supposed to be up there at all, getting in the

way. Now look what happened."

"No wonder she quit. And it's all your fault."

"She's a smart girl," Kitty said. "She knows when to get out."

Who were they talking about? Willow? Willow had disappeared this evening, too. Was that what Kitty meant by getting out? But what had Willow messed up for them? Had Willow fired the gunshots we'd heard? She'd been there. She'd admitted to riding up to the lake with Woody.

Kitty went on. "Unlike you."

"Uh-uh. I been practicing. See?" Blaze pulled something loose from a small case clipped to his belt and held it in front of the fire. A metal blade gleamed. It was a knife.

I faded back, deeper into my shadows, my gaze focused on the knife. It sparkled as he waved it, slicing the air.

"So what?" Kitty said.

"So I can hep you."

"You're in over your head, kid. Mitchell doesn't need your help."

"Oh yes he does. They're on to him. That detective and the whole bunch. I heard 'em talking at dinner tonight. Thought he'd like to know. You get my drift?"

"Don't do it."

"I want in. I deserve bein' in. And don't call me 'kid,' or else I'll tell everyone who you really are, Kirby."

Kirby? I held my breath, so that they couldn't hear me choking on my saliva as I tried to breathe, not that they were likely to hear anything in their half-inebriated state.

"You'll keep that to yourself," Kitty said, "if you know what's good for you. And I'll call you what I want."

142

Apparently I'd misjudged Blaze.

We'd been talking about poachers at dinner. That must be what Blaze was referring to now. This guy they were talking about... this Mitchell... he must be one of the members of the poaching ring. That's what Blaze "wanted in" on. Why on earth would they—or anyone—want to get involved in something so evil?

"No you don't," Kitty said. "You only think you want in, but it's not for you." She echoed my thoughts. "You've got yourself a future now. This place. You don't want to ruin it."

Money, I thought. Money drove them from innocence to evil.

"It ain't for me," Blaze said. "It's for her, see?"

Willow?

Kitty laughed softly. It sounded closer to a sob. "You'd risk all this for her? Man oh man, you're crazy, dude. It's too late for me, but not for you. You know what he's going to do to you if he ever catches you talking? And you *will* talk, kid, if you try to bring her in. He'll hunt you down to the end of the earth. Get it?"

I got it, just in case Blaze didn't. Not the specifics, of course. Just the gist.

This Mitchell they were talking about must be the poacher. Probably he was the very one Rosenquist had been hired to hunt down. Maybe he was Woody's killer, too.

And Kitty must work with him in the poaching ring. Kitty didn't have a twin sister named Kirby. Kitty *was* Kirby. One of those names was assumed, probably to protect her identity.

She needed protection now, if she'd seen what Mitchell had done to Woody.

Me too, now that I'd figured it out.

Master Hwang's voice replayed in my head. *The first lesson in self-defense is to avoid the situation. Run away!*

If they caught me here, lurking in the shadows, overhearing their secrets, what would they do to me? Would Blaze practice some more with his knife?

I crept backwards, hoping I wouldn't step on some crackling twig to give me away. Luckily, the rubber soles of my flip-flops cushioned my footsteps.

I kept going, fleeing through the thickest part of the shadows, cast by trees and various outbuildings. Halfway back to the front porch of the ranch house, I remembered Kitty's words about having a truck around back, waiting for "it," something that Mitchell would bring but couldn't find.

Blaze and Kitty were otherwise occupied with their beers at the fire pit. I could just take a look, couldn't I? Curiosity hadn't killed this cat yet. And besides, I never wasted time grabbing an opportunity when an opportunity presented itself. Mitchell wasn't here; that's what they'd said. If I hurried, I could beat him.

But even if he was here already, I wouldn't recognize him. Maybe Mitchell was a code name, and if I watched for him at the truck Kitty had waiting, I could find out who he was.

I needed to know. Blaze might not be in, but I was in way too deep to stop now.

I raced around the corner of the ranch house, following the curve of the driveway toward the barn. Starlight illuminated a truck sitting there, blocking the side door to the stables, the one Fiona had fled through that afternoon when I'd found her sobbing in the horse-stall office.

Sprawling junipers gave me cover as I crept closer. The rounded outline of the truck's bumpers gave it an antique look, like Woody's truck.

I peered closer. It *was* Woody's truck.

The last time I'd seen it was up at the lake. It had been parked off to the side of the fire road. Woody had apparently driven it up there, and now someone had brought it back here. Kitty. It must be the truck Kitty meant to use, to take delivery on something from some unknown person named Mitchell.

If Mitchell was the poacher, then the thing being delivered would probably be an animal. I hoped it wasn't the injured moose that had nearly run us down. The same one that maybe had run down Woody, according to the sheriff.

Oh gosh. Woody must have known that Kitty was Kirby. I was betting he'd been about to expose her. And then he'd died. I hesitated, thinking twice about moving any closer to the truck.

Then a hint of garlic breathed on the back of my neck. Fingers brushed my left shoulder.

Before those fingers could connect, I spun right. Years of training helped me react instantly, as if by second nature. I sidestepped away before garlic guy could fasten his grip on me. He was too slow. I danced on the balls of my feet and put up my guard as I whirled to face the lumbering shadow.

"Get back, dammit!" His whisper snapped at me. Rosenquist.

"What are you doing out here?" I said, relaxing my fists. I stepped closer to the junipers where he had been hiding.

"Keep your voice down."

I turned and looked at the truck. Kitty was expecting a delivery from the poacher. Rosenquist was investigating the poacher. He must know about the expected delivery, and he'd been staking out the truck when I got in his way. And then there was his possible connection to Kitty. I would find out what that was from my daughter. Soon, I hoped. Did he also know that Kitty was Kirby? Maybe that was why he'd dropped his armload of file folders back in the reception lounge when I mentioned her name.

"Is she working with you?" I said. I'd thought she'd been working with Mitchell the poacher, but maybe I'd figured it wrong.

"Why don't you give up and go back to bed, Mrs. Gannon, before you spoil everything?"

Well. He was right about one thing, but he had it backwards, as usual. I hadn't spoiled anything. *He* had spoiled it for me. Now how was I going to find out who Mitchell really was with Rosenquist breathing down my neck?

On the other hand, Kitty had been trying to keep Blaze out of whatever nefarious operation she was involved in. She wasn't exactly aboveboard, and neither was Rosenquist, but maybe they had things more or less under control.

At any rate, I could tell when my help wasn't needed. The warmth of my downy soft bed called. But I wouldn't give up.

"Okay, you win," I said, turning on my heels.

"Shhhh," he hissed at me.

I stalked along the driveway to the front porch, opened the door, and let it click faintly shut—*not* behind me. When I thought that he thought that I had actually given up—*no way!*—I dropped down to my haunches and duck walked across the porch to settle down in a shadowy corner and wait.

Chapter Fifteen

The next thing I knew, a lessening of the dark awoke me from my cramped position, hunched up against the porch railings. Darn! Not only had I fallen asleep while on duty, I was going to be a wreck today. My joints cracked as I straightened my legs and rose against impending dawn. A quick run would work out the kinks and revive me, then a shower. I limped back to my room to grab a windbreaker and my running shoes, laced them up, and let myself out again.

No one appeared to be about. Good. And I didn't have to worry about Jill's disapproval about my meddling because she wouldn't get up before noon unless I banged on her door.

The cold air of early morning was a rude slap, and I paused in the driveway to pull my turtle fur headband and mittens out of my pockets and slip them on. In the gray light of dawn, I scanned the driveway and the parking lot behind the pine trees. Willow's SUV, streaked with a light coat of frost, was still parked there.

The memory of the conversation I'd overheard between Blaze and my prime suspect Kitty, aka Kirby, topped off with a stalking Rosenquist, ran through my mind like a surreal movie. There was a distant quality to it, as if I'd dreamed it. Didn't I wish?

I patted my pockets, feeling for the small, hard shape of my mace canister. Check. Just in case Rosenquist was still out and about, waiting for an opportunity to tackle me. Or maybe I'd have to use it on a bear or a moose. I wasn't sure it would do any good, but it was better than nothing. In the martial arts, it's all about being prepared. And alert.

Then I set off slowly, my running shoes slogging through thick gravel. The crunching sounds I made crashed around me, and I thought my noise would surely wake up the entire ranch. Steering clear of the guestroom windows but not wanting to wander too far away from the premises at this hour, when wildlife prowled for breakfast, I set off down the driveway. The pearly pink sky of predawn lightened the surrounding hillsides with a soft glow.

Staying well away from the row of sheds and outbuildings—including the one that obscured the clay fire pit—I circled around the ranch house and headed toward the barn. No sooner did I turn the corner than I spied Woody's antique truck, still sitting in front of the stables.

Someone was lifting a tarp from the bed of the truck. I skidded to a stop behind the giant juniper where Rosenquist had tried to grab me only a few hours ago. The tarp dropped back in place, flapping over a bed that looked too empty to contain a moose. I breathed a sigh of relief, and then focused on the cowboy hat behind the truck. It was Blaze. He refastened the tarp and then stepped away from the truck. A delicately curved frame looped over his fingers and dangled carelessly as he moved. A crossbow.

I was pretty sure it was the same one I'd seen in the horse-stall office.

148

Blaze set off along the fire road, heading up the hill in the general direction of the lake. Where the moose hung out.

Mitchell must not have brought the moose in the night before. Perhaps he hadn't been able to find it. And now Blaze was going to prove his worth by finding it. Blaze wanted in. If he found the moose, it would all be legal with his crossbow, and he would redeem himself.

Not really wanting to witness such redemption, I decided to run the opposite direction. Spinning around, I headed back down the driveway, around the ranch house, past the outbuildings, past the parking lot behind the row of pines. The air was crisp, with no hint of smoke this morning. It would be another fine day in paradise.

I hadn't gone too far down the hill—a hill I would have to climb on my way back to the shower—when a stitch developed in my side. How annoying. I had barely begun my run, and downhill, no less. Pausing to pinch my side, I had just leaned forward and taken some deep breaths, when the rumbling sound of an engine made me look up. A vehicle crested the hill and pulled up to a stop beside me. It was one of those big rig 4 x 4's with tires up to my chest and an enclosed bed in the back. The driver's window slid down, and a hairy elbow poked out.

"Hey, you okay, miss?" said a man with shaggy hair hanging like a curtain that dropped around his neck. "You need a ride or something?"

I sure needed something, but it wasn't a ride with a stranger.

"No thanks, I'm okay." I massaged my side and straightened. "Are you part of the sheriff's team?"

"I reckon you could call it that." He snickered.

Had I made a joke? I didn't feel very much in a joking mood. "Well, then, you're here ahead of everyone else. You might have to wait. I don't think they've even got the coffee ready. Things are a bit off-schedule at the ranch right now."

He nodded. "I ain't making the coffee. That was Lillianne's job, but you don't see her here beside me, do you?"

I peered into the dim interior of the cab. The passenger seat next to the shaggy driver was empty. Was he still joking? "No sir," I said.

"That's 'cause she quit."

"She quit?" I echoed his words while my mind raced to catch up to what he was really saying. I'd heard those words only the night before, during that surreal movie at the fire pit. I'd thought Blaze and Kitty had been talking about Willow, but maybe they really meant Lillianne, the taxidermist's daughter. "Ah," I said, testing my deduction, "then, you must be Mr. McLean?"

"That's me. I usually bring her up here when she's working, and she makes the coffee. But she quit, so they're gonna have to make their own damned coffee this morning."

"Oh." What had Lillianne messed up that caused her to quit? "Are they expecting you at the ranch?"

"Better be."

"Oh yes," I said, remembering now. "Fiona told me yesterday that you were going to deliver a new trophy for their wall."

"It's not ready."

I shrugged, guessing that Woody's death had changed everyone's schedule. "I doubt if there's any rush now. Fiona wanted to replace one of the trophies for Woody. I gather some ratty old antlers—her words, not mine—went missing, and that upset Woody so much that he rushed out. I guess he thought he could find something better, but then, that didn't happen."

"Oh, it happened all right."

"It did?" I sucked in my breath. My face tightened as questions riddled my mind. I hoped he wasn't talking about a poached animal. Cautiously, I said, "But he had his rifle with him." And rifles weren't legal now. "Are you saying he shot something?"

"Can't say."

Can't or *won't*? That definitely sounded suspicious to me. I sighed, hoping to encourage McLean to reveal something. Anything. "Sadly, Woody never made it back, so I guess we'll never know."

"Yup," McLean said, not refuting the "never know" part.

"Do you think he meant to shoot his own trophy?"

"Nope. That'd be poaching, without a tag."

"I heard that Woody didn't care if his animals had been poached or not before they got stuffed to hang on his wall."

McLean frowned. "Where'd you hear that?"

"Maybe I misunderstood."

"I reckon."

This was going nowhere. I decided to be more direct. "I'm sure you don't work with any poached animals yourself." Actually, I wasn't sure of anything.

He snorted. "If I tried that in my shop, I'd be shut down so fast I'd be spinning from here to kingdom come."

A-ha! I tried to hide my smile and keep it from coming out as a know-it-all smirk. He hadn't ruled out not using poached animals somewhere *other* than his shop. But where? Did

Woody let him use one of his cabins for the purpose of dressing poached animals? Was that really why McLean had shown up here today, the morning after Blaze and Kitty were expecting a delivery from the poacher, someone named Mitchell? I had it all figured out.

But I wasn't as smart as I wished I were. I didn't know how I was going to catch them. I was pretty sure that Gustafson wouldn't cooperate with me.

Maybe if I kept up my direct assault, McLean would give me some ideas. "Do you happen to know a poacher by the name of Mitchell?"

His mouth rounded to a circle of surprise within the mess of his facial hair, as if I'd dealt him a blow he hadn't seen coming. "Who?" he said, choking.

"Mitchell. He's been poaching, and you should tell Officer Lester that."

"Nope. Never heard of him. Don't know no poachers, neither." A stony mask glazed over his face, and his jaw muscles clamped tight. A ruddy flush rose up his throat, as thick around as one of my thighs.

"What about Kirby? I'll bet you know someone named Kirby."

"See here," McLean said, narrowing his eyes at me. "I reckon all these questions mean that you're trying to tell me something, like where Rosenquist is at."

The way he changed the subject surprised me like a well-masked ridge hand that I hadn't seen coming. I staggered backwards a couple of steps. "Rosenquist?"

"You're working with him, ain't you?"

"H-hardly," I managed to stutter.

He squinted at me. "He said he's got a partner. That's you, I reckon."

I opened my mouth to tell him he had the wrong person, and then closed it equally quickly. Let him think what he wanted. Rosenquist did indeed have a former partner, and I knew him, although not as well as Jill did. Sean was a nice man. A good cop. "I know you recommended Rosenquist to the game warden to investigate a poaching ring," I said, "but did that also include his partner?"

"There sure is a lot of interest in Rosenquist, and I'll tell you what. He's fishing. Is that a crime?"

"Not that I know of."

"Me neither. Look, forget it. I'll just go on around back and find him myself. You sure you don't want a ride up to the house?"

I shook my head. "I wish you'd reconsider, though," I said. "About letting Lillianne join us in our workshop. Self-defense is self-empowering once you know a few simple moves."

"Exactly." He touched his fingertips to his forehead in a salute, scowled, and raised his window.

Didn't he want his daughter to be self-empowered? *Grrrr.*

The big vehicle lumbered forward. When its taillights disappeared around the next bend, I changed course. It wasn't the stitch in my side that made me turn around and head back uphill toward the ranch house. I was simply curious. I wanted to know what McLean was up to.

And besides, he'd gotten my hackles up.

No one had asked me, but I thought Fiona might appreciate it later if I kept an eye on this guy for now. For all I knew, he could be an imposter. Maybe he wasn't McLean at all. I'd put that suggestion in his mouth. Who wouldn't agree, if he was up to no good?

Jogging up the last of the hills before the ranch, I kept to the foliage of the trees. There was no use announcing myself. I wasn't sure what to expect.

What I didn't expect was finding nothing. I peered around the corner of the ranch house, where I had a good view of the stables and barn. Woody's antique truck still sat there, but McLean's rugged vehicle did not. It was as if the earth had opened up and swallowed it.

Not really. It was probably parked out of sight in one of the many outbuildings. But why hide it? These questions only added more fuel to my already perplexed mind. I glanced to my right and to my left. Over my shoulder. Straight ahead. No one was in sight. There was no hint of movement through the windows of the ranch house or over in the barn. Didn't ranchers have to get up early to take care of animals? The roosters were crowing. Where was everyone?

Not that I really wanted anyone to show up just now. Seizing my opportunity, I darted across the last of the driveway to Woody's antique truck, unfastened the tarp that tucked across the back, and lifted one corner. There was nothing inside except for a fluorescent orange piece of cloth. Woody's hunter's vest? Then, he hadn't been wearing it when he died because he'd left it behind in his truck.

Leaning over the side of the truck, I snatched up the smooth fabric. It was a vest, all right. When I lifted it, something small clattered to the metal floor of the truck's bed and rolled away from my reaching arms. Nestled into one corner, it was a small, brittle tube of grayed white, about the length of a finger. It looked a lot like the piece of antler I'd seen next to Woody's body.

Was it?

I was pretty sure it was.

Gustafson hadn't found it. That's why he'd been so evasive with me. He hadn't found the antler because it had been tucked inside the vest Woody hadn't been wearing.

Which meant that someone had moved the bit of antler there *after* my students and I had already seen it. A chill crept down my spine. Woody's killer had been watching us, waiting for us to leave.

* * *

After a shower, a change into clean workout pants and tee shirt, and a steaming mug of coffee, I felt better. Not great, but better. Questions still buzzed my mind, threatening to steal my focus away from the reason I was here: the workshop I had to lead. I reminded myself of my need to make a success of the workshop and to sign on new students to the studio down in Boulder, but my attention kept drifting back to poor Woody.

Did his killer think we'd seen him?

I tried not to worry about it as I banged on Jill's door. Or later, when a car bearing the rest of my students arrived. Two more young women, named Camilla and Chrissie. Somehow, we all made it through a self-serve breakfast, the washing up, and finally the workshop got underway. We would've had an even number if Kitty had shown up, as she'd said she would, but she didn't, so I had to fill in as one of the partners. Cleverly, I paired myself with Willow.

"We were worried about you last night," I told her as everyone found their own circle of space in the room and arranged themselves in pairs, "when you didn't come to dinner. Are you all right?"

She nodded and gave me a half-hearted smile. "I just felt a little under the weather. I'm okay this morning, though."

"Glad to hear it. You can't be too careful about altitude sickness."

"Oh, that wasn't the problem."

"No? It wasn't?" I wanted to hear more, but I couldn't take the time to coax anymore out of her just then because I had to lead the entire group through some basic maneuvers. "Let's talk at the break," I said.

With Willow as my prop, I demonstrated various types of holds and ways to release from them. Then everyone fell back into their pairs and practiced, switching off between the attacker and defender roles. For most people, it takes several trials before they remember the effective sequence of moves. They have to drill over and over until the split-second movement of grab-release becomes natural for them, knowing which way to step and turn and what to do with their hands. Willow, however, picked up my instructions quickly, giving me extra time to circulate through the pairs, correcting their twists and turns. I couldn't help wondering if Willow'd had some experience with these moves. And what was that problem she was going to tell me about?

The morning passed quickly amidst giggles and questions and comments, and soon it was time for our first water break. I caught up to Willow in the bathroom line. Yeah, that kind of water, too.

While I hoped to hear her confession, I certainly wasn't going to confess what Libby and I had learned the night before when we'd gone into Willow's cleared-out room. I knew that she'd simply packed up and left, but I wasn't going to remind her of that. For some reason she'd decided to come back. I was glad enough of that.

"So what's going on?" I said, giving her an encouraging smile.

Willow hesitated, and then she turned her head, facing away from Chrissie, who stood in line in front of us. She blurted it out in a burst of whispers. "I didn't want to mention it, because I thought it might be rude. And I thought you might not let me in. See, the truth is...well, I already take karate. I'm a green belt over at Kim's in Boulder."

My rival. Good school. I could've worked there, but then, I wouldn't have had the freedom to develop my own program the way Mr. Callahan lets me do. But that explained a lot. It was no wonder Willow picked up these self-defense moves so fast. "This workshop was open to anyone," I said. "It's not exclusive for my students only. In fact, no one here is signed on at my school. So that's not a problem at all."

Willow exhaled deeply, as if she'd actually been worried about it. "Well, it's more than that. When I found out you were going to hold the workshop here, at Woody's ranch, I couldn't resist. This is my favorite valley in all the mountains."

"You're familiar with this area, then?" I'm a native Coloradoan, but it was my first time here in this particular place.

She nodded, shifting in line. "TAfA has been doing some training camps up here ever since the moose population started to explode. We want to make sure they continue to thrive."

"How is this a problem that worried you?"

"It's not. It's just that…I have a friend who has a cabin down in the valley, about five miles away." She waggled her eyebrows at the mention of "friend."

"Ahhh," I said. "He's more than just a friend, right?"

"She."

"Okay." I remembered back to our introductions the day before. What was it Libby had said about her partner, Willow? Something about a divorce. Perhaps this friend was one of the reasons that had contributed to Willow's divorce.

"I wanted to spend some time with her," Willow said, "since she doesn't come down to Boulder very often. So I ducked out for a bit. Frankly, I didn't think anyone needed to know. And then, given the way that nasty sheriff treated me, and the way everyone was talking about killing animals, I almost decided to ditch this whole weekend. I wasn't going to come back at all. You didn't think I wasn't coming back, did you?"

"Why, no, not at all." Even to my own ears, I sounded too coy.

Willow didn't seem to notice my evasiveness as she went on, and we moved up in line. "I had to talk things over with… my friend. But in the end, she helped me realize that I needed to honor my original obligation to everyone, so I came back. And here I am."

"We're glad you did. You could've brought your friend, you know."

"I know. But she… Well, let's just say she doesn't get along with certain people around here."

Now she had my attention. "What do you mean?"

"It's that woman, you know? The one who has the horse here?"

158

"Kitty? What about her?"

"My friend remembers when she moved to the area a few years ago. Gossip said she was running away from a domestic abuse situation. They thought she'd killed the man, and then got off in a plea of self-defense. But my friend isn't so sure about that. She's just uncomfortable being around someone who's so potentially violent."

"Why'd you come back, then?"

"It didn't have anything to do with Kitty. I just thought it was the wrong thing, not to come back." She ducked away from me, as the bathroom became available.

So. I studied the closed door, and I thought my instincts had been right about Willow. She wasn't our killer. I only hoped Gustafson was equally convinced.

Chapter Sixteen

We took a two-hour siesta at lunch, not that we needed that much time to slap together our sandwiches. After we'd eaten and we all helped tidy up our mess in the kitchen—Fiona was nowhere in sight—the others disappeared back to their rooms. I slipped out the back door. I never have been the world's greatest napper.

Besides, I had a mission. McLean had miffed me about his attitude regarding his daughter. I had no intention of letting him get away with whatever he was up to. I intended to find out where McLean had hidden his big rig. And why.

Coasting around the corner of one of the sheds along the driveway, I heard the hiccuping sounds of a rattling engine, then the clang of something metal, alerting me to my subject's possible presence. Following the sounds, I rounded another corner and spied—not the big rig—but an old car sitting on blocks instead of tires. Its hood was up, and the back end of someone dressed in jeans bent over the engine, examining the way it sputtered and shimmied.

I paused to watch for a minute. The engine coughed one last time and then fell silent. The tinkerer straightened and backed away. "Dang it," he said, tossing a work glove to the ground. It was Blaze.

"Hello," I called out in a cheery voice. *Catch anything*

this morning with your crossbow? I was tempted to ask. But I bit my tongue before I could open mouth and insert foot. He didn't know I'd spied on him. I preferred to keep it that way.

He bent down to pick up the glove as if he'd merely dropped it, and by the time he stood up again, turning around, a crooked smile had pasted onto his face. "Howdy, ma'am." He glanced at his wristwatch and back at me. "You guys done already?"

"Not for the day. We're just on a break. We can't work as hard as you seem to do."

"Getting this old heap to run ain't part of my chores. I got to work on it during my lunch break. Uncle Woody said if I could fix her up, then I could have her. And I figured I'd better try while I still got the chance. Before...well, you know."

No, I didn't know. He was set to inherit the ranch, he'd told me, and that must include this old junk heap of a former car. All of this would be his one day. And that day was here. He sniffed, and I thought I understood. Tinkering was his way of dealing with his grief for the death of his uncle. "I'm sorry about your uncle," I said.

"Yeah, me too. But I reckon he's right where he wants to be, up there with Aunt Edna." His eyes rolled heavenward.

"It's a comforting belief," I said, not knowing what else to say. I wasn't a subscriber to any church, but a vision of cranky Woody stirring up a chorus of angels made me smile.

Blaze snorted. Maybe he'd had the same vision. "Where's the rest of your gang?"

"Taking naps."

"How come you're not napping, too?"

"I just wanted to go out for a little walk and..." See what

McLean was up to? "Clear my head."

"It need clearing? Usually, the mountain air puts our guests out like a light."

"Not me." Before he could quiz me further, I changed the subject. "About yesterday... When we met out there..." I waved vaguely in the direction of the gravel and dirt track between the house and the barn. "I knew what had happened to your uncle, but I didn't say anything. I was going to, and then something rang, and I missed my chance."

"It doesn't matter. I was fixing something, and it was ready. What you heard was the bell. Anyway, I already knew about Uncle Woody."

"You did?" But we had just returned from the lake where we'd found his body. How could Blaze have known that quickly? Then I remembered his argument with Kitty. She'd ridden back on her horse and arrived here faster than the rest of us. She'd told Fiona, and she must've told Blaze, too. "Kitty told you, right?"

His face darkened at my mention of her name. So they still hadn't resolved their differences.

I went on, trying to smooth out any ill feelings. "I didn't think it was my place to be the one to tell you. That's really why I was looking for Fiona. I thought it was her responsibility—"

"Everyone runs to Fiona!" he said, spitting on the ground.

I stepped back, keeping my toes dry from his little demonstration. "I only wanted to tell Fiona first about Woody."

"Yeah, that's always the way it is."

Well, maybe because *she* was the adult. But this probably wasn't the time to remind him of that. Instead, I said, "I wanted to let her decide how to break the news to everyone else."

"She coddles Kitty too much," Blaze said, his voice rising. "She thinks she's in charge, but she ain't, y'know."

"I didn't know." Who then, I wondered, was in charge? Blaze? He was hardly more than a teenager. "Kitty told me that Fiona practically runs the ranch, and so I thought…"

He made a growling sound as my words faded away, fading with the memory of his argument with Kitty, not only the day before but also at the fire pit. He'd wanted "in," and she'd called him a kid. He was too young, too naïve, too innocent to become a poacher.

"Yeah," he said, pulling on his gloves. "Everyone thinks that." He scowled as if he wanted to hit me, but he diverted his energy to the engine under the hood, and spun around to poke here and there.

Questions kept percolating in my mind, but I couldn't let him suspect my real purpose: snooping. "Look," I said to his back, "I'm sorry to bother you, but if it's not Fiona, then maybe you could tell me who really is in charge of the ranch now? You must know who it is, right? I need to talk to that person about our bill."

His head twisted around to look at me as his body remained bent over the engine. "There ain't gonna be no refund."

I guessed that meant he was that person in charge. "I'm not expecting one."

He glanced at his watch again. "Look, I ain't got much time. I got to finish up and get myself cleaned up for Lill." The back of his neck flamed.

Lill? Did he mean Lillianne? The nickname gave me the idea that he knew her pretty well. Well enough to have a crush on her?

164

His head ducked down, and his voice aimed at the engine before him. "You said everything you wanted to say?"

"No. Why was Mr. McLean here this morning if his daughter quit and didn't need a ride to work?"

Blaze lifted up from his tinkering and turned around to frown at me. "McLean came here?"

"That's what I said. I thought you'd know why, that is, if you and Lillianne..."

He stood up taller, scowling as he bumped his head against the end of the hood. "Did he bring it?"

"Bring what?"

"The new moosehead. He was fixing one up for Uncle Woody."

"He said it wasn't ready." Then a new thought occurred to me, and my heart raced with possibilities. "What's Mr. McLean's first name?"

"Huh?" Blaze said.

"His first name. He must have one. What is it?" I'd assumed Mitchell was a last name, but it could also be a first name. If Mitchell was the poacher, and if McLean stuffed poached animals... Could they possibly be one and the same person?

"I dunno," Blaze said. "Wait a minute. Fred, I think. Yeah, that's it."

"Are you sure it's not Mi—" *Oops.* I bit my tongue. I wasn't supposed to know that name. Mitchell. Let alone that the taxidermist's name could be Mitchell McLean.

Blaze's eyes narrowed, and he took a step closer to me. "Look, what's this about?"

I didn't want to let on that I'd overheard him talking with

165

Kitty the night before, expecting the delivery from Mitchell. The poacher. I thought fast. Distraction was my friend.

"Miffed," I said, "that's what. I was going to tell Fiona, because she's *miffed*, but maybe I should let you know instead. Some files were removed from the registration desk last night after dinner. I'm pretty sure it wasn't authorized by…the person in charge."

"What files? Who took them?"

I shrugged. "It looked like newspaper clippings. And it was Rosenquist. Mr. McLean was asking about him, so I was just curious."

"Dang it." He frowned and backed away from the car. "That cop was *here*?"

"I haven't seen him today," I said, matching his frown. Blaze seemed more worried about Rosenquist than the possibility I had discovered Mitchell's real name. "What do you suppose he wanted? They seemed to be articles about wildlife."

He scratched his chin and stared up at the trees. Either he was thinking about it, or there was an owl up there. "Probably has to do with that moose," he finally said.

"Moose? What moose? The one the sheriff thinks killed Woody?"

"It's not important. Uncle Woody always liked to collect newspaper articles about hunting, and there was one in particular about a moose that caught his interest." His gaze drifted down from the treetops and alighted on me, looking surprised, as if seeing me for the first time. "Now if you don't mind, miss, I got plenty of chores to do." Hastily, he released the prop and let the hood of the car fall with a slam. Then he took off at a gallop, headed uphill in the direction of the fire road.

* * *

After the siesta, I led my students through another round of drills. Jill didn't come back for the afternoon session. She needed a longer nap, but I suspected she was quickly losing interest in the workshop. She'd never fully appreciated "kicking and punching," but for whatever reason, that left me with an even number of students. Everyone paired up, and I got to supervise. I circulated around the workout room, calling out the moves, fixing my students' angles for ease of release. And then we did it all over again. Repetition, repetition, repetition.

Gustafson showed his haggard face just in time for the water break. The way he slumped made him look as if the stuffing from his teddy bear shape had been beaten out of him. Just like my students were beginning to look.

"May I have a word with you, ma'am?" he said, his finger pointing sloppily at me.

I nodded at him, called out "fifteen minutes!" to my students, and then led the deputy sheriff outside into the crisp, fall afternoon. I glanced uphill at the golden aspen and longed to be up there in their midst.

"How may I help you?" I said. *Here we go again.*

"I just have a couple things to clear up." He pulled his worn notebook out of his trouser pocket and thumbed through it to the page he wanted.

"Willow was away visiting friends," I said, carefully turning her secret liaison into an anonymous plural. "She didn't do it."

Gustafson ignored me as he studied what was written on

the page before him, flipped some more pages, frowned, and then looked up at me. "How long did you say it took you to hike up there to your picnic at the lake?"

I wasn't sure that I had ever told him. But someone had. Carefully, I said, "It was about an hour."

"Can you be more specific than that?"

I frowned, thinking, but at least Willow didn't seem to be on his mind. "Let's call it fifty-five minutes. We would've made it in less time if not for all our stops along the way. Why?"

"I'm asking the questions here. Did you see anyone else heading up there?"

"I already told you. We passed a couple other hikers, but they were going downhill."

"You sure they weren't hunters, who you saw?"

"I don't know who they were. We only said 'hello'. They weren't carrying rifles, and they weren't wearing orange vests like we were." But that just made them careless, not necessarily hunters. Or not. I wondered what Gustafson was getting at. Something about the sequence of events seemed to trouble him.

"You didn't see any horses?" he said.

A-ha. "No, we didn't see Kitty's horse."

His face crumpled into a mass of wrinkles. "You seen Kitty since yesterday?"

I thought about it. Should I tell him about the midnight rendezvous at the fire pit? If I did, it would get out that I'd overheard Blaze and Kitty, aka Kirby, talking. And if the killer learned that I'd been snooping, what would he do to me and my students? I wasn't sure they were quite ready yet to put their self-defense moves to a real test.

On the other hand, telling the sheriff, even a deputy

sheriff, was the right thing to do. I would have to deal with the consequences of the killer later.

"I might've... um... overheard Kitty," I said, "talking to someone."

"You *heard* her?" Steam curled around his words. "What did I tell you about not sleuthing?"

"Look," I said, "what's important is that I think she operates as someone identified as Kirby, and her partner is your poacher, some guy named Mitchell. Isn't that Mr. McLean's first name?"

"No, it's not."

I frowned. "Well then, do you know anyone else around here by that name?"

"Who told you that?" His voice thundered.

"Uh, no one."

"Is that what you heard Kitty say? That she's really Kirby and this 'Mitchell' she was referring to is the poacher?"

"Not exactly. I guess I... kind of guessed."

"You guessed?"

"Right. That's what I said. But look, it was pretty clear what they meant. They were talking about shooting."

"They? Who's 'they'?"

"Kitty—or Kirby—and someone else. It was dark." Blaze was a kid, and I always advocated for kids. I had to assume the best for kids. I wasn't going to send any of them to a future of crime, even if it looked like they were well poised on the path of delinquency. Bottom line, I wasn't going to turn Blaze in, just because he'd wanted "in."

"You could swear to this?"

"Well, no. I might've been wrong thinking it was Kitty,

but it sure sounded like her. You've got to find her. Either she's in on the poaching, or she'll clear all this up for you."

"And where do you propose that I look for her?"

"How would I know? I'm not the cop." His attitude was annoying me. "You better get to work... sleuthing."

He couldn't waste any time. If my suspicions were right, then the poacher had killed Woody, and he must've had help—from Kitty.

* * *

I thought about it the rest of the afternoon. My stomach quivered, and my knees turned to jelly. In my condition, I was not helping my students, so I called an early halt to the day's session. From their winded faces and their smothered grins, I gathered that they didn't mind.

I raced straight to the telephone on the reception desk. Terra should be home from school by now. She picked up on the first ring, which told me she was done booking and done with her test.

"How did it go?" I asked her.

"I didn't fail."

Which meant she didn't ace it, either. "Honey, I'm proud of you," I said, laying the groundwork for our next battle of wits when it came to homework.

"You just want to know what I found out online, don't you?" she said. My daughter always could see through me.

"Well, now that you mention it..."

"Here's the thing, Mom. You didn't tell me about the body."

"Body? What body?"

"'Fess up, Mom. It's all over the internet. Some body was found up there, run over by a moose. They haven't identified the vic yet, but I'll bet you know."

"Vic? Honey, you watch too much TV."

"Mom, you can't change the subject. So, who was it? I'll bet you know. You didn't just happen to ask me about moose attacks and Detective Rosenquist. So, what gives?"

I sighed. "All right, I'll tell you. But first, tell me what else you found."

Terra didn't answer for a while. I could picture her eyeball roll. Some clicking sounds came across the line as she was probably opening a window on her computer. She'd saved up for it from her half-time janitorial job at the karate studio. Finally, she cleared her throat and assumed a more efficient tone of voice as she reported her findings.

"It's like good cop/bad cop," she said, "just like on TV. See, the good part came when Detective Rosenquist rescued a Kirby Byrd from a domestic abuse case about five years ago. He found a safe place for her to stay. He never said where it was, but reporters found out it was somewhere in the mountains with her mother's best friend. That covers a lot of ground."

"No name?"

"Nope."

"You sure about that?" I could guess where—here.

"Listen, Mom, do you want what I've got or not?"

"Sorry, honey. Please go on."

"Okay, you were wrong about her sister. I couldn't find anything about any Kitty Robin."

"That's okay," I said. "I don't need that anymore. Tell

me about the bad cop part."

"Whatever. You remember that moose that wandered into downtown Boulder a while back and some cop shot it? Well, it was Detective Rosenquist's buddy. The guy shot it deliberately for the antlers, and Rosenquist swore that his friend had to shoot because it was attacking them. Rosenquist was the only witness, and he claimed the moose didn't die. That the bullet missed, and the moose got away. But later the cop who actually did the shooting confessed what really happened. He helped Rosenquist load the dead moose into his pickup, and then he drove it away to some guy he knew up in the mountains. It was somewhere he liked to fish, and this guy stuffed animals under the table. The police department ended up firing both of them. They haven't decided yet what the charges will be, but it's going to go to trial."

"Wow," was all I said. Then, after I thought about it some more, I added, "You found all that online?"

"Sure, Mom, it's all out there. You can find anything."

"*You* maybe. Not me."

"So, Mom, now you give. Who's the dead guy, and did the moose really do it?"

I glanced over my shoulder to see if anyone was near enough to hear me. I was in the clear, but I lowered my voice anyway. "Keep this to yourself, honey, if it's not public information yet. The guy was our host here at the ranch, and no, I don't think the moose did it."

"Huh," Terra said. "I knew it! So, if Rosenquist is up there, then I bet it's because of the moose. Sounds like you need some help solving your case of the moose-killer. Gramps and I can help. We can come up first thing tomorrow. I'll figure out a way to make him take us there, don't worry. Ice cream, maybe."

"Honey, no. Under no circumstances should you and Gramps come up here."

"But Mom—"

"No buts. Everything's under control."

She whined some more, and finally gave me a half-hearted agreement, and then we hung up.

Didn't I wish I could believe myself? Nothing was under control.

Chapter Seventeen

The rest of the day went downhill from there.

Somehow, we made it through dinner. Harlan and Andrea organized the entire meal, delegating tasks to all of us. Fiona, who was still absent—grieving, I suspected from the red puffiness of her eyes the last time I'd seen her—had told us to help ourselves to the supplies we found in the kitchen. Dinner didn't turn out to be the festive affair I had envisioned, back in the planning stages for this workshop. Surely, I wouldn't get any of these guys to sign on at the karate studio, not now. I figured my days were numbered there.

Nell, Nell... I could hear my sensei, Master Hwang's scolding voice in my head. *Get rid of negative thinking.*

Okay, okay. Sleuthing and body counts took their toll on me.

Jill didn't offer a nightcap, even though tonight I could've really used it. What a weekend this was turning out to be. I guessed she was either out of port or else she had a telephone date with Sean, her latest boyfriend.

I headed to my room alone. I didn't mind. I needed some alone time to wrestle some more with my unread book. But I kept listening for the coyotes, instead, or maybe for Edna's ghost. I didn't hear either.

I heard something else. A tapping sounded on my

bedroom door, as in knuckles gently rapping. I wasn't expecting anyone, but I had an idea it was Jill, back from her escapade and burning up to tell me all about it.

"Who is it?" I called out, in case it wasn't. You couldn't be too careful.

There was no answer.

I climbed out of bed and tiptoed across the room to my bolted door. "Jill?" I whispered. "Is that you?"

Jill would've giggled. There was no giggle.

I leaned close to the wood panel of the door and peered through the peephole. I had a clear view of the hall, even though the tiny fishbowl lens distorted my view, and the carpet runner curled up on both sides. No one stood there. Granted, the lighting was dim in the hall, thanks to a single nightlight plugged into a socket several doors down from mine, but I would've seen her, if she was there.

She wasn't there.

No one was there.

I reached for the deadbolt. *Wait, was this a trick?* My fingers stopped in mid-reach. *Someone* had knocked on my door. Where was he?

"Hello?" I called through the door. "Who's there?"

I thought I heard a floorboard creak. Whoever had been outside my door seemed to be moving away.

Without a moment's hesitation, I raced over to the nightstand where I kept my purse. There were no phones in these guestrooms, and my cell phone didn't work. I had no way to call hotel security, even if there was such a thing here. I guessed I was the closest thing this ranch had to a security force.

I dug inside my purse and pulled out my ring of keys.

They made a good weapon when splayed through fingers, but my key ring also carried a miniature stick. It wasn't an escrima stick, which I knew how to handle in order to incapacitate an opponent, but this midget stick was better than nothing. I could still use it to flick someone where it hurt.

With one swift move, I flung open the bolt and my door. I was pretty sure my visitor was long gone by now, but just to be extra cautious, I dove to one side, holding out my tiny stick for protection in front of me.

No big baddie stood there in the hall. No marines either, darn.

I would have to do this myself.

Where was Rosenquist when you needed him?

I poked my stick into the opening of the doorway, probing, and waited. Nothing moved out there in the hall. No hand grabbed the stick that I offered.

So I followed the stick's lead.

There was no one in the hall. No out-of-place shadows.

But something clicked. A door?

It sounded as if it had come from the end of the hall, where it emptied into the reception lounge. It sounded like the front door closing.

I padded softly down the carpeted hall, and as I moved, I tucked the keys from my ring between my fingers, transforming my fist into an iron studded ball. Too bad my feet were bare, and I was dressed in my nightie tee shirt. Oh well.

All was quiet in the reception lounge, and best of all, there was no one here. A tiny movement caught my eye. The lace curtain covering the glass inset of the front door swayed ever so slightly. The front door *had* just closed. I sniffed the air and thought I could detect the lingering smell of cigarette smoke. Yes, someone had been here, someone stealthy who'd wanted to alert me, and yet didn't wish to be seen.

The stealthiest person I could think of was Mitchell, the mysteriously elusive poacher, mainly because I'd never seen him. I didn't know if that's who'd been here, but if it was, then I wanted to catch a glimpse of him so that I could identify him to Gustafson and not only bring the poaching ring to justice but also maybe even redeem myself in the process.

I raced across the room and grabbed a throw from one of the couches, wrapped it around my shoulders, then headed back to the front door. It was unbolted. If Mitchell was indeed my nighttime visitor, then he'd entered with a key and hadn't bothered to lock up on his way out. Why not? Did he know I was onto him? Or maybe someone inside had let him in.

I didn't like it.

But someone had to do security around here.

I pushed the curtain aside and squinted at the dark night out there. The chairs on the porch sat empty, the rockers motionless. Nothing moved, not on the porch nor in the driveway. Slowly, I turned the doorknob and stepped outside onto the wooden floorboards. I left the door open behind me, just in case Mitchell got hostile and I needed to rush back inside and throw the bolt.

Standing there on the porch a few moments, I let my eyes adjust to the dark. No hulking shapes lurked nearby. A breeze stirred the air, murmuring through the pine needles that surrounded the ranch house. I wrapped the throw around my shoulders and crept barefoot down the steps.

Dancing on gravel in the driveway, I sniffed the air. There

was an unnatural smell, something acrid. It was the faintest hint of diesel fuel.

Willow liked to go out at night, visiting her friend, and her SUV was diesel. Was that what I smelled now? Had she been out again, and that's what I'd heard? The fumes still lingered in the air. Good grief. My nerves were on edge, and my imagination had gone nuclear, thinking Mitchell had lured me outside.

I took some deep breaths.

Calmer now, I realized how unlikely it was that Mitchell—someone I didn't even know but assumed was the stealthy poacher—would've teased me like this. Because, really. Even if he'd seen us up there at the lake, it wouldn't have taken him more than one glance at my shortness to decide that I couldn't present much of a threat. He didn't know me.

My fist relaxed, turning loose of my keys. But as I turned back toward the porch, I heard the horses nickering. Not just one, but several of them. That was unusual. Wasn't it? It was as if they were talking to each other. Soft thudding sounds of their stomping, shifting hooves told me that something had unsettled them.

I didn't think they would be disturbed by a vehicle's comings and goings. Did they have an instinctive distrust for anyone with animal blood on their human smell? I curled my fingers around my keys again and set off down the driveway for the stables. This time I steered clear of the bushes where Rosenquist had tried to grab me the night before.

Closer, I heard another sound, a mechanical one that didn't belong in this otherwise quiet night. It was the rattling purr of an engine. It seemed to be coming from one of the sheds across the driveway from the barn. In fact, it was the same shed I had used to shield me the night before when I'd eavesdropped on Kitty, aka Kirby, and Blaze.

Now, the double doors to the shed stood wide open.

An open door was like an invitation to me. *Come on in*, it seemed to say.

Nell, no be stupid, Master Hwang's voice rang in my head.

Probably not a good idea to confront a poacher who was also a murderer. He'd lured me here. Of course he had. That's why the horses were upset. And I'd fallen for that dumb old trick, just because my head had swelled large enough that I'd thought I was single-handedly the hotel force's security staff. Who was I kidding?

I stopped. Turned back to the cover of the bushes beside the ranch house. Looked again at the open doors to the shed. It was totally dark inside. I'd probably missed Mitchell. Again.

All right. I was here now, so deal with it.

And anyway, I could take him down.

As long as he didn't have a gun, that is.

Or a knife.

I knew a few moves against knives, but I really didn't want to test my skills—not again. Most of my practice had been with plastic, and those few times I'd gone up against real ones, hadn't turned out pretty. I still had the scars as reminders. I didn't need any more scars.

But I had to hurry before he got away. Or she.

And then what, Einstein?

I didn't know. But I was already speeding across the driveway toward the shed. So I kept going. Maybe I'd catch him leaving, and then...

Starlight lit the open areas, exposing me to anyone who might be watching. Feeling like a ninja, I hurried faster, the throw I'd borrowed flapping around me like large wings. When I reached the shed, I dove into the shadows beside it, plastering my body against the splintery siding. From what vantage point could anyone see me? Feeling bolder, I moved sideways, closer to the open doorway of the shed.

Rattling engine sounds floated out of the darkness of the interior.

I rounded the corner and ducked inside to the warmth of oily, diesel smells. Woody's antique truck was parked inside, filling most of the shed.

Packed dirt and loose pebbles pinched my toes. Some dark object lay ahead, sprawled on the ground in the narrow space beside the truck. I didn't think it was supposed to be there, whatever it was. Someone could trip over it. Me.

I paused to squint at it, puzzling.

I took a step closer. The thing didn't move, so I took another step. Then I recognized that one of the shapes extending from the shadowy mound was someone's leg. It was a person lying there, in a heap. And that person wasn't moving.

Chapter Eighteen

Dread washed over me as I lunged forward in the dark interior of the shed. "Are you okay?" I called out. Clearly, he wasn't. Lying in a heap on the hard-packed dirt floor beside the truck, with its engine running, was a pretty good clue.

He must've been about to jump into the truck and flee when something terrible happened to stop him.

I looked up into the darkness of the shed's ceiling, expecting something to fall on me at any moment. Nothing fell, and I saw no large object that might have struck this poor guy.

Was he Mitchell?

Or a Good Samaritan trying to save me from Mitchell?

Either way, whoever this victim was, someone had lured me here with a knock on my door, with intentions that I suspected were not exactly benign.

And then something had felled him—something that had really been meant for *me*. He'd gotten in the way of a trap set for me.

Or else this *was* the trap. Mitchell. The poacher. Woody's killer. My knees trembled as questions tossed through me, playing havoc with my mind.

He groaned faintly. I mumbled a silent prayer of thanks that he was still alive and dropped down to my knees beside...

"Kitty!" Up close, I recognized enough curves in the

semi-conscious lump to identify the cowgirl. "Oh my gosh! What happened?" What was she doing here?

The only answer she gave me was another groan. I didn't think she even knew I was there. It was too dark for me to see how serious her condition was. Not being able to answer me with anything more than a groan was a bad sign. I sprang to my feet and pounded past Woody's idling truck, over to the nearest wall that might have a light switch. Groping in the dark, I dropped my keys as my open palm slammed against the splintery wood. Finally, my fingers touched the slick switch plate. Light flooded the shed, used now as a garage for the puttering, antique truck.

Kitty lay face down on the dirt floor, crumpled where she'd fallen. It looked like something—or someone—had hit her from behind, knocking her out cold. Her arms tucked beneath her chest. Long strands of her hair splayed around her head, covering her face and curling around loose, dried leaves that had blown inside. They tangled in her hair, along with other bits of debris. Blood dribbled from the line of her jaw, pooled beneath her shoulders, and seeped into the dirt of the shed's floor.

Yanking the throw from my shoulders, I raced back to her side. I had to stop the flow of that blood, but I wasn't sure where her wounds were. I didn't dare move her to find out.

With the help of someone's lovingly crocheted work, I wiped gently, trying to tuck the soft throw around and under her. I wondered if a knife had done this to her—in particular, Blaze's knife. He hadn't liked the way she wouldn't let him "in." He hadn't liked the way she'd called him "kid." But he wouldn't go this far. He wouldn't have hurt her, would he?

As Kirby, Kitty had been expecting a delivery from

Mitchell the night before, which meant she couldn't also be the elusive Mitchell. Had Mitchell finally delivered it, maybe tonight? My gaze shifted to the bed of the truck, but all I saw from my vantage point on the ground was the truck's side. Something apparently had gone terribly wrong.

Footsteps thudded behind me, and Fiona's no-nonsense voice cried out, "What in the name of heaven—" She gasped and then sputtered. "Oh lordy! Honey!"

"I found her like this," I said, dabbing gingerly with one fuzzy corner of the throw. "She needs help. Call someone. Now."

Fiona didn't wait for any explanations, not that I could give her any. Without a word, she whirled around and darted across the driveway. There were stables over there. And a telephone. I remembered having seen one in Woody's horse-stall office.

I kept dabbing at the blood, hoping I wasn't doing more damage than good.

When footsteps shuffled behind me, I looked up. It was Fiona, back already. Her rounded chest heaved as she struggled to catch her breath. Her hands fluttered helplessly in front of her face.

"It...it don't work!"

"What?"

"The phone! It's dead."

"The phone?"

"The phone! The lines are cut!"

"But," I said, thinking *knives cut*, "everyone has cell phones these days." Had this been more of Blaze's handiwork?

"Not us. Reception is too bad out here."

185

"Well, someone must have a cell phone that works." I'd seen Rosenquist on his. And Gustafson. But they weren't here, and I couldn't remember if any of my students' phones worked. I'd come down on them pretty hard about using them.

"Woody never allowed them here on his ranch."

Woody... I'd thought Kitty had helped the poacher, maybe even helping him with such gruesome business as murder, but seeing her here like this, I realized she hadn't been involved. What seemed more likely was that Kitty had witnessed Woody's murder, and then the killer came back to silence her.

"If we can't call out," I said, "then we'll have to take her. Where's the nearest emergency clinic?"

"About five miles away." Fiona wrung her hands. "I shouldn't have brought her out here in the first place. But I had to take care of her, didn't I? She's my best friend's daughter, and she's like one of my own. I thought she'd be safe up here in the mountains, with me looking after her, where that jerk couldn't find her."

I really didn't need two patients. I couldn't work on Kitty's wounds and calm Fiona's hysteria at the same time, so I let her go on babbling about whatever guilt riddled her while I kept pressure where I thought was the source of the bleeding on Kitty's head.

"It's not your fault," I said automatically.

"Yes, it is. She was so afraid of that man..."

Which man? The one she'd been running from, or... Mitchell?

Kitty hadn't sounded very afraid of Mitchell the night before. Was it possible that she'd revealed something about him, maybe to Gustafson? She'd talked to him, even though she'd warned Blaze not to. And if so, then Mitchell had done this to her as a show of force. Maybe Fiona knew him.

"Who was she afraid of?" I asked with a shudder. Being Kirby was dangerous to one's health.

"Her ex-boyfriend's brother," Fiona said with a sob. "That's who." She fell to her knees beside Kitty, pushing me out of the way. "He swore he'd pay her back for what she did to his brother. Is that who done this to you now, honey?"

The domestic abuse case was history. But how tonight's events might have played out now flashed through my mind...

Kitty had been riding her horse by the lake. She hadn't just found Woody's body, as she'd reported to Fiona, but she'd actually witnessed Mitchell in the middle of killing him. Maybe she tried to intervene, tried to save Woody, and then her horse became frightened—as the horses were frightened now, judging from the distant sound of their whinnies. Butterscotch had reared up, trying to strike Mitchell but had struck Woody instead and injured her forelegs in the process. By then, Woody was already dead.

Kitty's head lolled to one side, exposing her face, which grimaced. Her lips twitched as she moaned. It sounded like *noooo*.

Encouraged by her movement, I jumped to my feet and said, "We need to hurry. He might come back."

"How are we going to get her there?" Fiona wailed.

"We'll take Woody's truck," I said. "It's already running. We'll put her in the back, where she can lie down. She'll be more comfortable there." The throw wadded around Kitty could work as a sling to lift her up into the bed. We could make it work.

"You know how to drive that thing?"

"How hard can it be?" Lifting Kitty from the ground would be harder. I didn't even want to question whether or not there was enough gas to get us where we had to go.

"Nooo..." Kitty whispered, her lips barely moving. Weak, but her voice sounded loud and clear to me. "Didn't know..."

I leaned low over her. "You didn't know? Know what?"

"Not..."

Maybe she meant "know" instead of a negative. If my flash of inspiration was how it had really happened, then Mitchell couldn't allow Kitty to live. She could identify him. Because she *knew* who he was and what he'd done.

But she hadn't said anything when the rest of us were busy reporting Woody's death. Her silence had made me suspect her, but I was wrong. She must've been afraid for her life. She'd pretended surprise when all along she was afraid of what he'd do to her if she talked. That's why she'd kept quiet.

"But...her..." Kitty struggled to say.

"It's okay," I said, smoothing her hair off her face. "We're going to get you out of here. You're going to be fine."

If she was truly afraid, then she wouldn't have come back here tonight.

But she had.

My reasoning had been all wrong. I wasn't thinking straight. And no wonder, the way my heart was pounding. I felt dizzy, on the brink of hyperventilating.

Kitty hadn't been afraid of Mitchell last night at the fire pit. Either she'd been pretending, or else there'd been nothing to witness at all. If that was true, then Mitchell hadn't killed Woody.

But then, who had?

Blaze?

Blaze hadn't liked Kitty very much, and he was angry or maybe even jealous of Fiona over that little matter of control of the ranch. Was that enough to justify murder? And attempted murder?

Murderers, in my experience, had not needed much provocation.

"Butterscotch," Fiona said. "That's what she's trying to say."

"The horse?" I hurried around to the back of the truck where I fumbled with the latch to pull the end down. There was some junk piled in one corner of the truck's bed. We would have to scoop it out to make room for Kitty.

Fiona looked past me. "He got the wrong one."

Then I noticed the antlers. They hadn't been here before. Now, Woody's orange hunting vest was gone, and in its place was a pair of antlers, broken apart into several pieces and littered across the back of the truck. I recognized the signature shape of the flattened scoop of a moose. Tips had snapped off, and what remained of the jumble was streaked with stains.

Bloodstains. Maybe this was what had hurt Kitty just now. Her attacker had thrown his weapon into the back of the truck.

But Fiona's words sank in, and I tore my gaze off the antlers to look back at her. "What do you mean," I said, "by the wrong one?"

"It was Lillianne he was after. Not Kitty."

"What makes you so sure?"

"Because of Butterscotch. It's all my fault. I let Kitty down. I let Lillianne take Kitty's horse out for a ride yesterday, without Kitty's permission. I just didn't think..." Sobs choked off her words.

Because of Butterscotch, everyone—including the killer—thought Kitty had witnessed Woody's murder. When all along, it had been Lillianne instead. No wonder she quit work here. That's what had made Blaze so mad.

Just then, the double doors to the shed slammed shut, first one creaking bang and then another.

Chapter Nineteen

"Hey!" I shouted, springing away from the rear end of the truck and its rattling muffler. Something clicked from the outside—a lock clicking shut—as I slammed my body against the wooden doors of the shed. The doors didn't give.

"What's happening?" Fiona cried, crouching beside the truck where Kitty lay.

"Nooo," Kitty whispered from the dirt floor.

"No worries," I said, "I'll get us out." I backed away from the double doors a couple of steps and then lunged again, swinging my back leg up and twisting it around to my front. Leading with the heel of my foot in a back leg sidekick, I used all the torque and strength of my hips, along with the momentum of my lunge. Following through with an extended jab, I visualized my foot splintering through the wood of the shed's doors.

It wasn't enough. The doors held firm.

How long before the truck spitting exhaust fumes into the closed-up shed would asphyxiate us?

I'd turn off the engine long before that could ever happen, but still, we needed to get out. Kitty had an appointment with an emergency clinic. I kicked again. And after that, I used my other leg, which wasn't dominant. Just in case, I tried a front leg sidekick, then a thrusting front kick. They had less torque, and consequently, less power, at least for a superlightweight woman like me, but trying made me feel better.

The doors still didn't budge. They didn't even crack.

We couldn't afford to test the length of time we had, nor how many kicks it would take for me to finally break through. I couldn't risk accidentally running over Kitty if I tried reversing the truck through the doors. I sprinted around to the driver's seat of the truck and reached in to switch off the ignition. The shed fell silent, but fumes filled the air. I didn't think this place was airtight enough that the remains of the exhaust could poison us, but I didn't want to take that chance, either. The exhaust had already been filling the shed even before the doors had closed. We needed some fresh air, and we needed it fast.

"What are we going to do now?" Fiona said with a sob.

"You sit tight with Kitty," I said, glancing around the clutter of the shed. "I'll find a way out."

I didn't see a single tool I could use. This place looked more like a storage room, lined with stacks of burlap bags and barrels of sand. But it did have a small window, a dark pane of glass high above one of the stacks.

Since I'd dropped my keys somewhere in the clutter by the light switch, I grabbed the first alternative that was handy— some broken antlers from the back of the truck. They looked as if they'd snapped off of a mount. I wondered if these were Fiona's missing, ratty old antlers, and why they'd been in the back of Woody's truck. Grateful to have something—anything—I gripped the broken stalk tightly and crawled up onto the pile of bags. Burlap and barrels shifted beneath my feet as I climbed, but at least the stack didn't collapse. Reaching the window, I beat against the glass pane with the antler.

It worked. Glass showered in a spray of shards out into

the night. Where a fire burned. For an instant, my heart leaped. Then I recognized the fire pit, and I settled back into simple alert status. It wasn't a wildfire out there but small, contained flames in the clay fire pit. That was okay.

No, actually, it wasn't. We still had to get Kitty to the clinic. I had to get the truck through those barred, double doors, and I preferred not to have to do a Hollywood stunt. Sure, I could use the truck to ram through the doors, but I didn't want to move Kitty anymore than necessary. Besides, I was thinking of something less destructive. On the other hand, maybe destruction was preferable to cutting my bare feet on the pool of broken glass outside the window. That's when I caught the scent of gasoline.

Then I saw someone. *It must be the killer.* He'd been out there all along, watching. Our lights. Our movement. Waiting. A hooded figure, holding a can, bent over, sprinkling its contents onto the ground in a little demonstration meant just for me. He sprinkled in a line from the back wall of the shed toward the fire pit. *Oh. My. God.*

Gasoline!

He was going to set the shed on fire. Once his trail of gasoline reached the fire pit, it would all ignite. He'd meant to trap us inside.

Nightmares about fires, set especially to trap me, still haunted me.

Tell me this isn't happening again, Jill's voice whined in my head. I remembered last month too well.

But I'd handled it back then, and I could do it again.

"Hey!" I yelled, clutching my broken antler and swinging one leg through the open window, moving before thinking. All I knew was that I had to stop him. Hesitating, you lose the point.

Diving foot first through the open space of the window, I only vaguely noticed the jagged edges of window glass scratching through my tee-shirt nightie, slicing my thighs. My leading foot sailed through the air, and my flying sidekick took off big time. All too soon, I landed with a thud onto the dirt, shuddering from the jolt through my body, but not feeling the glass that must be cutting through my calluses. In one swift move, twirling and leaping with the force of the tornado kicks I'd spent years practicing, I sprinted away from the pile of broken glass. The antler in my grip threw me slightly off balance, but I still managed to land a bloody foot against the camouflage print of the killer's hoodie jacket.

He stumbled backwards, but he didn't fall.

Uh-oh.

The times I'd had to use my sidekicks against opponents had always sent them to their butts. Not this time. This guy's core was so solid that the impact of my foot against him almost made me lose *my* balance. I staggered just a bit.

Jeez.

This guy was like a brick wall, and while I had, in fact, split a brick once under Master Hwang's supervision, I'd never taken on an actual wall of bricks.

Footwork! my sensei's voice reminded me in my head.

Dancing on the balls of my feet, I backed up, out of the killer's reach, buying a fraction of extra time while I considered another approach. At least I'd stopped him from sprinkling anymore gasoline. Yay. He tossed the can aside, and a deep chuckle rumbled in his throat.

It was a voice I knew only too well.

"Well, well, if it isn't Mrs. Gannon." Rosenquist. Rosenquist was a cop—maybe not such a good cop—but he wasn't a killer.

Was he?

Oh god. No wonder he was more formidable than all the rest of my opponents put together. Rosenquist was like a brick wall.

"Are you crazy?" I said, my footwork dance fading. "What are you doing out here with that stuff? Don't you realize there are innocent people inside that shed? Aren't you supposed to protect us? Or at least, go after Mitchell? He's the poacher. Why don't you do what you were hired to do?" As soon as my tirade was out of my mouth, I realized my mistake. I'd been wrong about Mitchell.

It was Rosenquist. It had been him all along.

"Not as smart as you thought you were, are you?" Rosenquist said, apparently enjoying my flummoxed state.

I wanted to curl up in a ball and cry. All these months, ever since Max walked out on me, this cop had been on my case. I should've known all along that somewhere along the line his mind had twisted. He hadn't just been making my life hell, blaming me for Max, accusing me of doing away with him. This guy had lost a screw somewhere. He'd gone over the edge, fallen into the pit of corruption. For whatever reason, he meant to take all of us out.

No way.

I had to keep moving. I had to keep him talking, but not too long. I couldn't waste time. Kitty needed a hospital. Staying on the balls of my feet, I circled around him, first one way and then the other, drawing him away from his gasoline trail. Could I get to the switch in time and turn off the fire pit? That was the key, wasn't it? Keys... I thought hard. *Darn!* I'd dropped my keys.

All I had for a weapon were the antlers that I clutched. These half-rotten pieces of bone weren't exactly a bo staff nor a pair of kamas nor chuks, but I could make them work, could turn them into my own newfangled martial arts weapon. I had to time this carefully.

"Not as smart as you," I said, going for the approach that would hopefully soften him up. "You were always way smarter than any other cop."

"About time you recognized that, Mrs. Gannon. You've been in my way since the get-go. Convenient, that you came up here where I can finally take care of that little problem once and for all."

"All this was for me?" Using my peripheral vision, I kept him in sight and mentally calculated how many more steps I needed to reach the switch for the fire pit. Eliminate the source of ignition, and the fuel of the trail would be useless.

"Don't flatter yourself."

"I just don't understand why you threw it all away. Your career. You could've been chief of police."

He screamed with rage.

I must've hit a sore spot.

Maybe not my best idea, tormenting an already enraged bull.

"Those punks!" he shouted. "Wet behind the ears! They get all the favors instead of us guys with experience."

"I know what you mean," I said, trying to soothe him. I edged closer to the fire pit. "It's the same in my field."

"I took him on as a rookie, and what thanks do I get?"

"Sean Hennesey?" I said. Jill's most recent boyfriend.

"That damned punk stole my job. He *poached* it!"

"You're an expert at finding poachers," I said, buttering him up. *Ick.* But I was another step closer to my target.

"He tried to tell me I was doing it wrong. Me! What does he know?"

"Not as much as you." One more step.

"You gotta know when to rough 'em up, I always say, before they rough you up."

"The way you roughed up Woody?"

"You never quit, do you?" His voice growled again, a warning that I'd pushed too hard.

"Only because," I said, my stomach turning, "I can't help but admire your...dedication. Fortitude." Enough, already. "I only want to know how you do it."

Another step.

Rosenquist chuckled. The way he glowed from my praise must've blinded him to my advance on the switch to the fire pit.

"All right," he said, "it won't hurt to tell you, 'cause it's the last thing you'll ever know. You won't get away from me, see?"

"I know when I'm beat," I said, gripping the antlers with sweaty palms.

"It's just that Woody was going to make a big deal about that moose down in Boulder. Said he had 'evidence'."

"Those newspaper clippings?"

"It was nothing. He collected shit. But the punks were already after me, and I could've lost my pension, see? I couldn't let Woody rat me out."

"Of course not. You didn't mean to kill him."

"Damned right. I just meant to teach him a lesson. That old man would've been pleased, the way I made it look, like his dying was on account of a moose stomping him. Hell, he didn't live long enough to appreciate the irony. Died before I could poke him good. With those antlers he'd thrown into his truck. Now you just hand them over, so I can get rid of the evidence."

"This?" I said, thrusting the antlers up between us. "You want this? I'll give them to you." Handling them like an escrima stick, I thrust hard against him. But unlike the actual martial arts weapon, this piece of antler curved against the brick wall of his chest. The antlers snapped into pieces.

Only a stub remained in my fist as he grabbed me, whirling me around. My mind blanked. Before I could recover enough to release from his grip, he'd circled his arms around me, my back against his chest, and lifted me off the ground.

Not good.

This was a classic bear hug.

All the years of my training drained from my head in that one instant, as if I'd never learned a single move of self-defense. I squirmed. I wrestled, I screamed, I flailed my legs, all of it to no avail. He only gripped me tighter. His arms felt like a steel trap closing around me, pinning my arms to my side.

Think!

My heart beat too erratically, overriding my muscle memory. I'd repeated release techniques over and over, drilling them into my large muscles so that my gross motor skills would automatically make me move. Releasing should come as if by second nature, whenever the need arose. That was the theory.

Apparently, I hadn't practiced enough.

Breathe...

The cramp loosened from my mind.

Loosen him up! The training voice commanded in my head.

I kicked backwards, against his shins, but he didn't loosen. He was still a brick wall.

Then the memory of the sequence flowed through my body, an unstoppable torrent. *Turn head sideways, hands together, exhale, drop!* With the side of my chin pressed against his chest, my lungs collapsed of air, and my arms tightened close together, I made myself into a smaller package. My sudden move threw his center of gravity off balance, and I became too slippery for him to hold onto.

Pressing my advantage, I elbowed the brick wall, causing him to loosen his grip on me enough that I could slide free. Rolling to the ground, I shot out a sidekick into his groin. He doubled over, letting out an *"oof!"* of surprise, and I bounced away before he could recover enough to grab me.

This made him even madder.

"Wha-a-at?" he said with a growl of rage. "That's. Not. Possible." He lunged after me, but he was too slow.

My feet stung, and I moved faster. He might be a brick wall, but I was lighter, and I sprang out of his reach. Close enough to the fire pit. But where was the darned switch?

"You're dead," he said.

"Not yet." We circled each other, eyeing each other in the dark. I gripped the stub of the antler, and it was as if an elixir flowed through me, like the power of the moose, that enormous, gorgeous animal who'd maybe transferred some of his strength into tiny me.

I didn't really believe it, but there was no denying the power of positive thought. And anyway, I could use whatever help I could get.

I didn't waste time thinking. He was off guard, unsettled from my moves, and I pressed harder. Charging with the stub of my antler like a guiding torch, I blitzed him. The antler, my punch, and one of my feet all landed on him pretty close to the same time. He fell backwards, and I sailed over his head, yelling, "Ha-saaaa!"

"Hold it right there!" a voice bellowed. A spotlight flashed on. Searing light banished the dark. "Don't move, none of you, you hear?"

I heard. It sounded like Gustafson. My pal.

"What in blazes is going on here?" the sheriff shouted.

About time you showed up, I wanted to say. Luckily, I bit my tongue.

"Nell? Nell!" Jill squealed and darted into the light, toward me.

"Ma'am!" Gustafson shouted. "Get away from there."

A pair of deputies scurried into our circle, their guns drawn on Rosenquist. Handcuffs snapped around his thick wrists while Gustafson read him his rights. Another deputy switched off the fire in the fire pit.

Before they could lead him away, Rosenquist called me some names I couldn't repeat. He'd always wanted the last word.

I grinned back at him. Yes, I'd definitely earned the title he gave me.

Chapter Twenty

Thirty-six hours later, not too long before check-out, my students lined up in the driveway under the direction of my organizing daughter. She and Dad arrived first thing Saturday morning, despite their promise not to come.

But they were too late, darn. They'd missed all the action.

Terra turned her attention instead to organizing this little display. It was some sort of graduation ceremony, and it had been my students' idea to show off—I mean *demo*—their new skills. Empowerment beamed from their faces as they paired off and went through the series of grabs and counter maneuvers that I'd taught them over the weekend. The rest of us watched their performance from the comfort of the ranch house porch.

"Pretty cool," Blaze said, his arm around Lillianne as they glided together in the porch swing.

"I wish I could've taken that workshop," said Lillianne.

"There's a class kind of like it on the other side of the pass," said the game warden, Officer Lester, from one of the Adirondack chairs.

"Want me to drive you over there to check it out?" Blaze said. "I'm gonna have a new car real soon."

"You made that old thing run?"

Blaze laughed and winked at me. "It's all in knowing how to do something."

Wasn't that the truth? Luckily, I knew a few self-defense moves, which had ended up saving the day for all of us, but this young man was a mechanical genius. Apparently, he was the one who'd "borrowed" Rosenquist's truck the day Woody died up there at the lake, jump-starting it to slow Rosenquist down. It almost worked.

"Young man," said Gustafson, swiveling around from his position leaning against the porch railing, "I'd say you know too much for your own good."

"Yes sir," said Blaze.

The deputy sheriff grinned. "And now that you have a ranch to run, with more than a little help from Fiona, you're going to be mighty busy."

Blaze grinned back.

"Too busy," Lester said, "to get mixed up in any poaching ring."

"I guess I don't need that anymore." Blaze gazed adoringly at Lillianne.

"Son," Gustafson said, "you just keep on keeping your eyes open and your nose clean, and you're going to do just fine. Woody was always proud of you."

"Yes sir." Blaze's chest swelled just a bit, and with good cause.

He'd proved that there really was a poacher named Mitchell. The day after we caught the killer—Rosenquist—Blaze had single-handedly tracked Mitchell—the poacher—to his campsite. That's where Gustafson surprised him, nailing him for hunting with no tags.

Two arrests, in as many days. We were all flying pretty high, but me, most of all. I had four signed contracts in my hands, and Rosenquist was finally out of my life for good. He'd turned out not to be any different from the poachers he was supposedly investigating. He'd seen himself above the law. Power had corrupted him.

"Don't you get too busy," Lillianne said, tickling Blaze in the ribs. "You promised to teach me how to use your crossbow, remember? If I'm going to use it again, I don't want to mess up and end up hurting anything, like I did on that poor moose."

"Aww, he's okay," Blaze said. "You didn't hurt him. He's tough."

Tough and powerful. Somehow, I'd made a connection with that moose, or one like him, and it had given me the extra ounce of strength and power I'd needed to finally overcome my nemesis. Or was it just the power of positive thinking, as Master Hwang had tried to teach me all along?

My students looked good, including Jill, who went through the moves with the devotion that only she could give it. All of them had learned a lot in only three days. They wouldn't have had the chance, if not for Jill, my sis. Jill had known something was wrong when she tried to use the telephone on the reception desk to call her boyfriend, Sean, and figured out that the lines had been cut. Despite the spotty cell phone reception, she managed to get a text message to him, and he called up Gustafson, who arrived in the nick of time with his cavalry.

Gustafson turned to me. "You were lucky that one of you didn't get hurt when Rosenquist fired those gunshots to scare you off."

"What shots?" Dad said. "Nellie, you didn't tell me about any gunshots."

"It's all over now, Dad." Ever since they'd arrived, Dad had been sniffing for the trouble he always wanted to fix for me. Thank goodness, he was too late. I implemented my distraction technique. "Didn't Terra do a great job planning this show?"

His attention turned to his granddaughter, out there on the driveway. She could do no wrong. His face beamed, and he led a round of applause.

Not everyone had been able to make it here today to this performance, though.

Kitty had been airlifted down to Denver, and Fiona had gone with her.

Mr. McLean was busy tending to paperwork. Something about tags and straightening his books.

Best of all, Rosenquist's bail request had been denied.

I felt the tension drain from my shoulders. They'd made me sit in the center chair, with my bandaged feet propped up.

"Well," said Doc Newman with a laugh, "everything turned out well, didn't it? Kitty's going to be okay, and no one else got hurt. All things considered, we're pretty lucky."

Lucky? I wasn't so sure about that. Self-defense techniques took a lot of work and even more practice. But this group of new students was ready and willing to work. And I was eager to work with them.

*****

Nell Letterly's Self Defense Tips

Sometimes amateur sleuthing will land you in trouble. If, like Nell, you are a magnet for trouble, then here's a review of five basic safety tips from *Murder by Moose*:

1. Avoid Trouble: The best defense in martial arts is not to have to use any defense techniques at all. Don't hike into gunfire during hunting season.

2. Stay Positive: The power of positive thinking will keep you from looking like a victim. When you are positive, you look more confident, and that keeps you safer from thugs. They prefer easier targets than someone who looks positive and confident that she's safe and secure.

3. Stay Alert: If you have to go out after dark when mountain lions are on the prowl, stay away from bushes and shadows where thugs like to hide. And take something with you for extra protection, like pepper spray or maybe a stick.

If avoidance and positive thinking and staying alert don't work, and someone grabs you by the arm:

4. Release that grip! Pull your arm in the direction of the assailant's thumb. No matter how strong a thug is, his thumb is never strong enough to hold you one-handed.

Or if someone wraps his arms around you from behind:

5. Release from a bear hug: Turn your head sideways, so that the side of your chin presses against your assailant's chest. Clasp your hands together, which draws your shoulders in. Exhale, releasing air from your lungs. These actions make you a slightly smaller package for the assailant to hold. Do them quickly together and drop, slipping out of your assailant's grip.

Good luck, have fun, and remember to stay safe!

About the Author

Sue Star writes mysteries about families in chaos. She is the author of the Nell Letterly mystery series. Like her character, Sue has also trained and taught the martial arts, but unlike her character, Sue believes her life is more stable. She enjoys hiking, traveling, and just hanging out with her family.

She also writes stand-alone short mystery stories and has collected several in *Trophy Hunting* and *Organized Death*. *Trouble in a Politically-Correct Town* contains stories about Nell Letterly's friends. With Bill Beatty, Sue also writes suspense with a touch of romance in exotic settings and is the author of *Dancing for the General*. She is currently hard at work on the next book, tentatively called *Burning Candles*.

Find out more about her writing at dmkregpublishing. com.

Follow Sue on Facebook, Twitter and Goodreads.

Contact Sue at suestarauthor@gmail.com

Sue STAR

www.ingramcontent.com/pod-product-compliance
Lightning Source LLC
Chambersburg PA
CBHW070009260626

47159CB00005B/1738

* 9 7 8 0 9 8 9 3 5 7 8 8 3 *